UTAH HELL GUNS

UTAH HELL GUNS

STEVE FRAZEE

THORNDIKE
CHIVERS

This Large Print edition is published by Thorndike Press®, Waterville, Maine USA and by BBC Audiobooks Ltd, Bath, England.

Published in 2005 in the U.S. by arrangement with Golden West Literary Agency.

Published in 2006 in the U.K. by arrangement with Golden West Literary Agency.

U.S. Hardcover 0-7862-7964-8 (Western)
U.K. Hardcover 1-4056-3583-5 (Chivers Large Print)
U.K. Softcover 1-4056-3584-3 (Camden Large Print)

The text of this Large Print edition is unabridged.
Other aspects of the book may vary from the original edition.

Set in 16 pt. Plantin.

Printed in the United States on permanent paper.

British Library Cataloguing-in-Publication Data available

Library of Congress Cataloging-in-Publication Data

Frazee, Steve, 1909–
    [Range trouble]
    Utah hell guns / by Steve Frazee.
        p. cm. — (Thorndike Press large print Westerns)
    Originally published: Range trouble. New York :
    Phoenix Press, 1951.
    ISBN 0-7862-7964-8 (lg. print : hc : alk. paper)
    1. Utah — Fiction. I. Title. II. Thorndike Press
    large print Western series.
    PS3556.R358R36 2005
    813′.54—dc22   2005015299

UTAH HELL GUNS

—CHAPTER ONE—

The clack of steel wheels striking rail joints can say almost anything, depending on what lies in the mind of the listener. To Reno Keegan, riding west across desolate lava flats in a sowbelly coach, the rhythmic sound above the fish plates was an endless repetition of *Need help! Need help!*

Keegan wondered what brutal urgency lay behind those two words that had taken him from a mining claim he was guarding with a rifle at Kokomo, Colorado, for they had been from his father, who years before had said he never again wanted to see Reno.

Three months after Appomattox young Reno Keegan had run up the gravel walk and leaped the two steps to the porch of his Illinois home. Square-jawed, red-headed Liash Keegan had seen him coming and had met him on the porch to deliver a bitter opinion of the kind of son who would sneak away to fight with rebels against his own father and brother.

Liash Keegan ended with, "Always

remember — you fought side by side with men that killed your little brother."

Till then Reno hadn't known about his brother. He went white and a dozen memories of a little red-headed boy rose to make the smash of his father's words more brutal.

"Get out," Liash Keegan said quietly. "From now on never say you're my son. Get out."

Between those words and the terse appeal that had come a few days before lay years of loneliness and wandering. Young Keegan did another hitch in the army, fought Indians on the plains; he learned the shifting, muddy waters of the Missouri and spent three years as a steamboat pilot; he cooked his bread twisted on a stick over a fire of buffalo chips during trail herd drives from Texas; and then he'd turned to hard-rock mining.

In letters sometimes delayed for months Keegan's mother worked patiently to reconcile father and son. She kept each informed of the other's whereabouts, probing gently, tirelessly to find a time-opened breach in the barrier between them.

She tried until the day she died.

Beside her casket father and son avoided

each other's eyes. Still bound by his own false pride, Reno glanced sidewise at his father once and thought he saw a sign of softening; and then the old man, gray showing now in the dark red of his hair, turned stonily away.

They parted without speaking, the younger Keegan going back to Colorado to try his luck at mining once again; the father returning to his construction company somewhere north of Ogden.

Two months later the message came in a letter two weeks old — two words, his father's signature, and the address: *Keegan Construction Co., Beyond end of track. Oregon Short Line.*

Reno Keegan hadn't hesitated, though he had a solid grip on his first piece of good fortune in mining.

And now the end of the rails was not far ahead.

Keegan stirred restlessly on the lumpy seat of the airless, filthy coach. By sitting straight and craning he could barely see through the narrow windows. Outside was barren lava rock, heat, sagebrush, and rolling hills.

He shifted weight and put one foot on a canvas barracks bag that bore his name in red paint.

Beside him a keg-chested man about Keegan's age stretched his legs into the aisle and yawned. "This coach was worn out when the Pennsylvania sold it — unless the conductor was lying and it was made by Indians to torture prisoners."

Keegan's grin lightened the lean soberness of his brown face and made little ridges at the corners of his gray eyes. "What would you guess it is to Yankee Falls now, Walker?"

His companion studied him with naturally healthy, unprying curiosity. "Maybe thirty miles," Walker said without shifting his eyes from the appraisal.

Keegan was lean to the point of apparent thinness, but the wide wrists showing beyond the sleeves of his faded corduroy coat were not bony. Though he had felt the solidness of Keegan's shoulder when the swaying coach flung them together, and even though he knew Keegan's exact weight as a result of an idle moment the two had spent near a platform scales at a station in Wyoming, Walker was still wondering where Keegan stowed two hundred pounds.

This black-browed man whose dark curly hair was cut unusually short for the prevailing style of the era had puzzled Walker ever since the two became acquainted as traveling

10

companions in Cheyenne.

Mainly it was a look of controlled tension about Keegan's wide mouth; a tenseness that lingered in his eyes for an instant whenever he brought his mind from his own thoughts to something in the immediate present.

More than one passenger in the coach had given Keegan keen appraisal during the last two days and nights.

Four or five travelers whose tenure of business — even life — depended on accurate grasping of human character had studied Keegan quite closely. They noted that he wore no gun; that his hands were hard from use; that in spite of an obvious eagerness to make the train move faster, there was a deep quietness behind his gray eyes.

Walker had seen that quality too. He had wandered much where spaces are big and free of the noisy clatter of human beings, and now he was drawn toward Keegan by a feeling that they both had shared mutual experiences.

"You may as well go on to Oregon with me, Keegan. Big valleys, plenty of water, rich land — they say you can't beat it."

Though he had not chattered about his business, like several in the coach, Walker had not denied that he was doing the same as a dozen others in the hot, crowded car: getting free transportation west to the railhead on a promise to put himself and his team to work for a construction company.

"Thanks, Walker," Keegan said. "But I'm still figuring to hit one of the grade-building crews beyond the end of the track."

Pins and links rattled. They shortened with crashes; took up slack with violent jerks as the three coaches and three freight cars followed the engine up and down the undulating grade. The worn wheels called their words to the rail joints.

Over and over in Keegan's mind the noise said: *Need help! Need help! . . . Killed brother! Killed brother! . . . Get out! Get out!*

He twisted his lean body. "I'll be glad to get out of this cage," he said.

"A railroad ought to go some place," Walker said. "This one just goes." He sighed. "I'm longing to light for good when I get to Oregon." All the longing of the homeless wanderer was strong in his voice.

A half-hour later the engine stopped as if sudden death had struck it down. The dusty seats and dusty passengers went forward with grunts. Bleary-eyed sleepers roused and cursed.

Keegan strained to look out a narrow window smeared with grease from coal smoke. He saw a red water tank and a small cluster of tents and green lumber shacks. Walker was peering over his shoulder.

"That engineer must have decided to stop after he was halfway past," Walker said. "He probably sprained both front legs."

Keegan grinned. "Let's stretch," he said.

He followed Walker down the aisle. They stepped over the legs of bearded sleeping men who long ago had become adjusted to crashing stops. They crunched the remains of shoe-box lunches, rattled empty whisky bottles, and squeezed past a disorganized card game.

Morning sun laid hot fingers on Keegan's head as he swung off the platform. He squinted at the sunlight and breathed deep of the freshness of the hot, dry air, wondering why anyone had bothered to put windows in the sowbelly coach. You couldn't see from them and they didn't open.

He saw a station shanty thrown together from fuzzy yellow lumber that was fighting hard against its nails. A few loungers were sitting on sleeper timbers in the shade of the water tank. Off to the right the tents and warping shacks seemed uninhabited, drearily waiting the day when heat, wind and rattlesnakes would take back their rightful heritage.

"Judging from this place, you'd never know a railroad was being built," Walker said. "Give me Oregon."

They started following other passengers toward the water tank.

The man who came walking up behind Keegan seemed to project his presence before him by some subtle, unseen antennae. His feet made little sound but his very nearness seemed to exude a cold, dry whisper.

Keegan turned his head quickly and looked into a pair of ice-blue eyes that seemed deadly cold against the warmth of a lean, weathered face. There was gray in the sandy hair showing below the man's temples. He wore an unfringed buckskin jacket, slick and shiny where wear had been greatest, and his feet were clad in moccasins.

The man was fully as tall as Keegan, lean and quick-moving, with a suggestion of Indian background in his easy carriage.

14

He looked Keegan up and down with two flicks of pale eyes. For a moment they were shoulder to shoulder, and though Keegan never saw a lip movement he plainly heard the hoarsely whispered words: "Tent in back of hotel."

The tall man moved on ahead, then turned and walked briskly toward the collection of tents and shacks.

Keegan stopped, wondering if Walker had heard the message; by the latter's politely incurious expression Keegan knew he had.

Walker grinned. "I'm going down and find a leak in that water tank." As he started away he spoke without looking back. "If you miss the train I'll leave your loot with the agent in Yankee Falls."

Keegan stepped away from the stream of passengers walking past the coach and watched the buckskin-clad figure move toward the largest structure in the little camp, a part board, part canvas habitation. He waited a few moments and followed.

A bullet-riddled sign high on a post that formed one upright of a hitching stand identified the Shiloh House. Two horses and a mule were tied to the rail in front. As Keegan strode ahead he saw the tall man who had spoken to him reach one corner of the wooden part of the hotel and slump against it like a warm candle, apparently uninterested in the entire world.

But Keegan knew those cold eyes were weighing his every movement.

He went past the hitching rack and around to the other side of the hotel. Blocked from view from the railroad by a squat frame building, a small tent sat at the back of the hotel, its wall guy ropes anchored to short pieces of rail.

Keegan paused before it. The flaps were tied wide open. He looked around him for a moment before ducking into sickening heat under the canvas.

—CHAPTER TWO—

Liash Keegan lay under a dun blanket on a canvas cot. His face was shiny with the heat of fever, his eyes unnaturally bright and piercing. His hair seemed streaked with twice as much gray as Reno remembered seeing the last time he and his father had been together.

Liash tried to raise his head. "Hello, son."

The words killed for all time the last vestiges of bitterness from events long gone. Reno took two steps and grasped the hand that came up from the dun blanket, cursing himself instantly for the heavy pressure he put on limp fingers.

It struck him that his father's voice had been as feeble as his handshake. He knelt beside the cot, and Liash Keegan rolled his head to look into his son's face.

"I'm shot up a little, Reno. But I was all right when I wrote you, so don't think I was out of my head."

Reno waited.

"I don't know who it was," his father

said. "Whisper Jim is bent on taking me east to get fixed up. Don't worry about that part of it."

Liash moistened his dry lips. He read the look in the eyes of his son, who was thinking of the long, jolting train ride to reach a competent doctor.

The old man's cracked lips parted in a weak grin. "I'll make it, don't you worry. And I'll be back to help you when I can." He tried to get on one elbow, and Reno pushed him back gently. "The outfit is just about knocked stem-winding, son. I bit off a piece of work that fooled me, but that isn't the main trouble —"

He closed his eyes and breathed in quick, shallow gasps.

"Maybe you shouldn't be talking," Reno said.

Liash opened his eyes with an effort. "I got to. I got to tell you what I can — and that's not much. I could've licked the work, but all the dirty, underhanded, haywire things —"

He rolled his head from side to side and stared with feverish eyes at the sloping canvas above. "One thing after another. Somebody trying to wreck the outfit. If it was the job to fight I could understand, but —"

"Don't excite yourself now." Reno's gray eyes were grave as he looked at the shiny, flushed face.

"The devil to pay every time you turned your back. . . . Every fresno scooping up trouble. . . ." Liash Keegan was muttering to himself.

Reno's face was grim as he stared at his father. Never in his life had the son heard Liash Keegan complain that anything was too big or too tough to be handled — until this moment.

He listened to his father mutter words and phrases that meant nothing to Reno. Then Liash took another grasp on coherency. "Run that job, son," he said. "Core McLean has got all the papers you'll need to take charge. You can trust McLean."

"Maybe I'd better stay here —"

"Don't waste time with me! You can't do anything here." Liash's glare was not all fever. "Get started!"

Young Keegan stood up. "Who's the tall man outside?"

"Whisper Jim."

"Who's he?"

"I don't know!" Liash said impatiently. "I gave him a hand once a few years back. He popped up a few days ago — right after I was shot."

Questioning his father would be a waste of time and do the old man no good, Keegan decided.

He heard the train pulling out. He stood looking at the wounded man, loath to leave.

Some of the old man's harshness welled up when he saw his son's hesitation. "Forget about me and put out on that job!"

Keegan was lowering his head and shoulders to pass between the flaps when Liash called. He turned to see that his father had raised himself a few inches off the cot and was holding the position with terrible effort.

"Son, it wasn't the fix I got into that caused me to send for you — not altogether." He hesitated, his arms trembling from the effort to hold his shoulders up. "Many a time your mother said I'd see things different some day. She said —"

They looked at each other, each wondering why he had let the years slip by in bitterness, thinking of the patient, loving toil a woman had expended to bring them together.

"We'll start from here," Reno said.

Liash smiled. He fell back on the cot. "Good luck, son. I'll be with you soon."

Reno turned his face away to hide his doubt.

Free of the dead weight of heat inside the tent, Reno squinted in the bright sunlight and looked around. Whisper Jim had shifted his position and was now on the other side of the hotel. Keegan went over to him.

"You're going to stick with him?" Keegan asked.

Whisper nodded slowly, his ice-blue eyes studying Keegan without expression.

"What's the main trouble in camp?" Keegan asked.

Whisper moved his head from side to side. "I don't know."

His voice was the same hoarse whisper he had used on the first time he spoke at the train. "Liash got shot when he and some others were bringing a payroll into camp."

"Did that have anything to do with the trouble he tried to tell me about?"

"I don't know anything about the construction job," Whisper said. "No use to guess, is there? Just remember that anybody will make a try for a payroll." The cold eyes studied Keegan's face. "Got a good gun?"

Keegan nodded, listening to the fading sounds of the train. "How far is it to Yankee Falls?"

"About eighteen miles." Whisper Jim inclined his head toward the front of the hotel. "Bear Trap's out there — the one with a McClellan." His eyes and tone plainly hinted that he knew Keegan was no stranger to a McClellan saddle.

It struck Keegan that Whisper was a man who probably knew a lot of things that he talked about only when it suited him to do so.

The tall, buckskin-clad man glanced toward the front of the structure as if to say that time was passing.

"How come you're this far from the track heading?" Keegan asked.

"I loaded Liash into a wagon filled with hay and tried to catch the train after we missed it in Yankee Falls." Whisper looked again toward the front of the hotel.

Keegan glanced toward the small tent. He could hear his father talking feverishly. "Let me know how it goes with him."

"Trouble! Nothing but grief!" Liash Keegan's voice came strongly.

Whisper's nod was a barely perceptible jerk of his head. He walked quickly toward the tent and Keegan went out to the hitching rack.

The dusty brown mule that bore the shiny black leather of a McClellan saddle tried to remove Keegan's hand with a vicious snap of yellow teeth the moment its head was free. Keegan took up slack when the mule's long neck snaked back and held the animal's head twisted back while he mounted quickly.

Bear Trap relaxed, content to know that no amateur was taking liberties, content to express its satisfaction by soundly nipping the rump of a startled horse. Keegan swung toward the tracks.

A few men still loafing in the shade of the water tank watched with little interest the lean-backed man riding away on a dusty mule, headed west on a rocky road that ran roughly parallel with the railroad.

Out here men came and went and their business was their own — until it interfered with someone else and his pursuits.

Heat lay heavy on the nameless camp, which in a few months was destined to be marked by nothing more than dry fragments, tin cans, empty bottles, and a well that had supplied the camp and water tank.

Now the rails were falling farther and farther west. Beyond them lay trouble that had made hard-bitten, rugged old Liash Keegan mutter querulously.

His son rode toward it.

The mule set its own pace and Keegan was content to let it do so, feeling the familiar hardness of a good saddle beneath him once again. Out here was space to think and air to breathe and only the fact that he had lost a little time detracted from his relief at being free of the cramped and dirty coach.

His father, Keegan thought, must have been more affected by his wounds than he had at first believed. The old man had sounded rational enough at times, but now it occurred to Keegan that he had learned very little from Liash — and nothing at all from Whisper Jim.

He thought of his father's words about Core McLean being one man you could trust.

Bear Trap went on with long ground-eating strides.

At sundown Keegan rode into Yankee Falls. The sight of the gleaming Snake River made him want to strip his clothes and plunge in to scour the grime of dust and travel from his body.

He went instead directly to the railroad station, riding past sidings where only half the spikes were driven to hold rails that would soon be moved. Men were piling ties and rails on a work train pointed toward the wooden bridge across the Snake. Along the tracks for a quarter of a mile the ground was piled with supplies — hay and oats, bridge timbers, wagons, bales and boxes.

All around the station and the town beyond he saw and felt the stir of movement, the confusion, the stumbling and waste and apparent aimlessness that accompany war and large construction jobs.

Three painted women were standing by a piano loaded on a freight wagon, yelling shrilly at the teamster; a well dressed man in a beaver hat was arguing with a railroad employee about a broken whisky barrel, while a few paces away two bearded teamsters sat smoking pipes while resting on sheet metal kegs of black powder.

Near the station Keegan tied Bear Trap to the back of a freight wagon with a broken wheel. He went inside, half expecting to find Walker waiting there for him.

In spite of the heat the heavy-set man who rose from a desk to face Keegan across a high counter wore a double-breasted coat of dark wool that rested hard on his shoulders, dragged down by the weight of a gun in each pocket.

"A friend left a bedroll, a warbag and a

rifle here for me," Keegan said. It did not occur to him that Walker might not have followed his promise. "R. Keegan — it's painted on the warbag."

The agent studied Keegan with a long, level scrutiny. "The stuff is here all right." He watched a moment when Keegan began to feel in his pockets for his father's letter to use as identification.

"That's all right," the agent said. "You fit his description — the thinnest man that ever weighed two hundred pounds."

The heavy-set man continued to study Keegan.

"Well?" Keegan asked.

The agent stooped behind the counter and hoisted Keegan's gear, laying it on the planks. "That's the size of it, ain't it?"

Keegan nodded.

"You've got a team and wagon to haul it with — now," the agent said. He held the steady inquiring look of Keegan's gray eyes. "Your friend was killed. Before he died he told me to turn over his rig to you."

The agent shook his head and his eyes hardened. "He left your stuff here and walked toward the end of the platform where eight or ten drunken toughs were shooting in the air to scare tenderfoot passengers. One of them accidentally shot him."

"Right after he stepped out of here?"

"Just the time it takes to walk to the end of the planks."

Right after carrying in my warbag with my name in red letters all over it, Keegan thought.

"Who were these drunken toughs?" Keegan asked.

The agent scowled. "Just part of a crowd of one or two hundred people milling around to watch the train come in. With all that gunfire, nobody seemed to know who shot your friend, and if anyone actually saw the man they're not likely to talk about it. Maybe somebody bumped his arm; maybe he was so drunk he didn't know what he was doing."

The devil he didn't, Keegan thought.

Cold and hard as a ball of ice inside him, the thought began to grow in Keegan that Walker had been killed deliberately by someone who had mistaken him for Keegan.

He began to untie his warbag.

"I got his personal stuff in the back room," the agent said. "He gave me a name and address where to send it — a cousin back in Iowa, I think it was. There'll be some money left over —"

"Send that too," Keegan said. He took a

single-action Colt's revolver from his pack. He set a box of cartridges on the counter and began to load the gun.

The agent nodded approvingly. "The place is full of all the hangers-on and toughs you always find around these jobs. There's been six, seven payroll robberies between here and the camps." He paused. "That where you're headed?"

"That's the place." Keegan shoved the gun inside his belt. "You didn't recognize any of those men who were shooting?"

"I wasn't out there." The agent sized up Keegan's compactness of muscle and quiet gray eyes. "The team and wagon is down by the freight shed. Tom knows about it — ask him."

Keegan nodded. "How far to the end of the track?"

"She ends just a little ways across the bridge — where the engineers' camp is. From there on it's rough."

"That's what I've heard." Keegan gathered up his gear and started out. "Thanks," he said.

—CHAPTER THREE—

Bear Trap snapped twice as a matter of principle while Keegan was loading his gear on the mule.

Not far from the station Keegan saw what must be the freight shed, a tin roof surrounded and almost buried by piles of supplies. He led the mule toward it.

He stopped where a stooped gray man was driving down spikes that had started to work loose in shrinking ties.

"Hear you had some excitement?" Keegan said.

The old man rested on his maul handle and studied Keegan. "Yeah."

"See it?"

The railroader nodded. "Plenty. Too much."

"How's that?"

"I see one of them drunks cut down a-purpose on this young feller standing on the platform. He had one of them cheap bulldog guns — looked like a Prairie Giant or a Little Demon."

"Do you know the man?" Keegan asked.

The railroader shook his head quickly.

"Would you know him again if you saw him?"

The negative shakes became more violent, and then the old man turned his head away. "It ain't none of my business," he said.

"You told me part of it," Keegan said. "The man —"

"That's all I aim to tell." The railroader began to drive spikes. "There's no law here and it ain't healthy to tell everything a feller knows."

Keegan frowned, debating whether to try for more information or move on. The old man had sounded truthful — but he could have been making up a yarn to gain attention. If he *had* been telling the truth — Keegan was inclined to think he had — it might take a great deal of time and persuasion to make him say more.

If Walker's death had been a result of his being mistaken for Keegan, and directly involved in the trouble old Liash had tried to outline, whoever was guilty no doubt had gone his way by now, thinking his purpose accomplished.

Possibly straight back to Keegan's camp. There was the place to find the root of the trouble.

He went on to the freight shed, working his way around and between stacks of canned goods, baled hay, barrels of kerosene, green lumber and other stores. Judging from the congestion of goods, freighting must be quite profitable, Keegan thought.

Teamsters and swampers volunteered help in assembling the wagon. A short time later Keegan was moving behind a big team of iron grays, Bear Trap coming along on a trail rope. From a storekeeper who sold his goods directly from cases on the floor Keegan bought a few cooking supplies.

And then he headed west.

After crossing the Snake he stopped in the willows and undressed. Standing tall and lean in knee-deep current near the west bank, he lathered himself white and washed in the icy water. Men on a work train chuffing across the bridge laughed and yelled at him.

He waved one long arm at them and went on scrubbing until the last trace of travel grime was gone. While the hot sun dried him quickly he rummaged in his gear and changed to fresh clothes, vowing never again to go a full week without taking off his boots.

He cared for the animals, noting that the gray team was wobbly from its long train ride. He fried bacon, made hot bread and boiled coffee. Finishing with a can of peaches, he tossed the tin into the river and watched it go bobbing in the current while water slaps brought it lower and lower until it sank.

A short time later he was moving west once more, controlling an urge to force the team a little faster. Every time he looked at the well matched big team ahead of him he thought of Walker and the simple longing in his voice when he said: "I'm going to light for good when I get to Oregon."

In doing a simple courtesy for another, a man whom Keegan had begun to like and respect had lost his life. Keegan knew he owed a debt to Walker far greater than the value of this team and wagon.

Some way he would try to repay it.

The white tents of the engineers' camp began to grow larger. On beyond he saw a work train and heard a distant clatter of rails and the sounds of mauls striking steel. Directly ahead of him, in a sparse growth of scraggly sage before the tents, a man was shooting. The sound of his shots was loud in the still, hot air.

Keegan drove toward him.

The gunman was a squat youth wearing a fringed buckskin jacket and a wide-brimmed black Mormon hat. Propped against a sage brush twenty or thirty paces away was a round cardboard separator from a cracker barrel. It showed no holes.

The youth stroked a feeble blond mustache and waved at Keegan. "Go west, young idiot!" he cried, grinning. "You another boomer that got a free ride this far toward Oregon — or are you really going to work?"

Keegan grinned at the lad's brash good nature. "I'm going to try to work. How far to the grading crews?"

"Don't disturb me," the youth said. "This is my day to stay in camp and check notes. Watch!"

He fired at the cardboard target and missed it by at least two feet. He shook his head, wet one finger and raised it in the still air. "Very bad cross wind!"

Keegan grinned. "Regular blizzard!"

The shooter spun his weapon by the trigger guard. "The grading crews? That's hard to say. They go busted and move out so fast that we can't say whether a given company will be on the job from one day to the next."

"I'm looking for Keegan's outfit."

The engineer pointed his gun carelessly toward the target. The weapon bucked and a black spot appeared high in the cardboard. "Hell on a handcart!" he said, staring at the gun. "I thought it was empty!"

"Where's Keegan working?" Reno asked.

Still staring at the gun in his hand, the engineer said, "You got a long haul, brother. What's left of that layout is about halfway to Shoshone — if they haven't blown up in the last few days since I been out."

"What do you mean — what's left?"

Something in Keegan's tone caused the sharpshooter to forget his unloaded gun. "Old Liash Keegan got shot in a payroll robbery — they tried to rob him, that is — and now I hear the company is falling apart.

"It takes a bale of pick handles and a tub of guts to run an outfit on this job. Old Keegan had the stuff, but I hear he was having all kinds of trouble with his men." The engineer studied Keegan. "You better try Capps. He can pay off."

Trouble with the men; financial difficulties — that still wasn't enough to whip Liash Keegan.

"Want to sell the mule?"

Keegan shook his head. "I may need him to pack a bale of pick handles."

All flippancy was gone from the youth's attitude as he studied Keegan's face.

"Ever hear of Whisper Jim?" Keegan asked.

"Heard of him — yes."

"What's his business?"

The engineer shrugged. "Outlaw. Trapper — or something. Nobody seems to know." He grinned. "As far as I know nobody ever grabbed him by the shirt and shook him till his teeth chattered and asked him his business."

Keegan grinned. "Thanks for the talk." He spoke to the horses and drove on.

As the mule passed, the young engineer reached out to slap its rump. Bear Trap did a creditable job of snapping, but the rope brought him up a few inches short. The youth fell back in alarm.

"I'm glad I didn't buy that turtle!" he yelled.

Keegan drove several hours after dark, trusting the horses to follow the trace. Though he knew there was no forage, he picketed the animals so they could roll and lie down.

He rose from his bed in the wagon at dawn and was moving again before an hour had passed, following the tracks of countless wheels that had scraped and ground against the lava plains before him.

Off to his right he saw long stretches of grade completed except for bridges across gullies. Here and there rock formations rose in ragged formations to break the barren sweep of lava flats. He began to pass construction camps where teams and men were fighting shallow cuts.

At almost every camp someone rode out with an offer of work.

He was resting the horses at noon when a girl in a light spring wagon drawn by two black geldings came rapidly along the backtrail and overhauled him. She waved and started to drive past. Then something in the wagon caught her attention and she stopped.

She could be from a dance hall, Keegan thought at first; but no woman he had ever seen in a dance hall let her face get sunbrowned or wore a red bandana to bind her hair in public. This girl was also wearing a blue gingham dress. Her eyes were dark brown, not bold but frankly curious.

She wasn't exactly a raving beauty, Keegan decided, but still —

"Looking for work?" she asked.

He grinned. "You run an outfit?"

Keegan had a reasonably good opinion of his looks, even when badly needing a shave; but he thought her scrutiny went beyond normal interest. "I figure on working for Keegan," he said, studying her face.

"Why Keegan?"

He grinned. "Because that's where I want to work."

She smiled. Her eyes joined her lips in the expression and Keegan reduced his estimate of her age from twenty-four to twenty, making also certain other revisions of his first opinion of her looks.

He was grinning in return when her face went serious again, leaving him with a feeling of being trapped with a silly smirk on his face.

"How far to Keegan's camp?" he asked.

"About five miles on. You go over Coyote Hill, pass Capps' outfit — that will be the biggest camp you've seen so far — and the next one is Keegan's." She glanced again into the wagon box behind the gray team.

"That's right," Keegan said. "The name is mine."

"The son who went south when he should have stayed north?" she asked.

"I see you know my history."

"I live in your father's camp. My Dad has been blacksmithing for your father for years."

"I forgot your father's name," Keegan said, frowning.

She smiled. "Grieve. Mine is Laraine."

"Grieve?"

She nodded, still smiling. Keegan cautiously boosted his opinion of her looks another notch.

"What's wrong in camp?" he asked suddenly.

Her smile disappeared. She studied him thoughtfully. "I could tell you part of the troubles but you'll find out when you get there." For a moment he thought she was going to say something else.

Then she lifted one hand and drove away. He saw that the spring wagon was carrying a fairly heavy cargo lashed over with a tarpaulin. "Let *me* tell 'em I'm coming!" he called.

—CHAPTER FOUR—

Keegan ate cheese that had been a long time coming west; he munched dry crackers and washed the lumps down with juice from another can of peaches. As he flung the tin away he thought that if he ever got rich his trail through life would be marked by empty cans that had held peach halves.

He used his hat to give the last of his canteen contents to the gray horses, ignoring non-working Bear Trap, who retaliated by nipping one of the horses on the shoulder.

Before he reached Coyote Hill, which was no more than a rock-strewn, steep little bulge in the lava plain, he passed a twelve-team high-wheeler towing two wagons loaded with hay. A short distance beyond he overtook a slow-moving tank wagon driven by a bearded teamster who grunted surlily in reply to Keegan's greeting.

Hauling water great distances, freighting supplies from the railhead, battling tough lava rock with scrapers, handicapped by the average contractor's optimism over probable yardage in relation to money owed — no wonder men worked under difficulty in this country, Keegan thought.

But he knew that it was more than any of those problems or any combination of them that had made rugged old Liash Keegan, even though wounded, mutter and complain.

At the bottom of Coyote Hill Keegan unhitched and took his team up to help a tank wagon that was having trouble. The teamster, a long-necked weathered man with a wild mustache, provided a doubletree, a long chain and profanely pungent comments on the idiocy of people who wanted to build a short line to Oregon or any other place.

On top of the hill he gave Keegan water from a cool bag and scowled at a lame off-wheeler that had thrown a shoe sometime before.

"They're saying they'll have rail through here in thirty days," the teamster said. "We may never live to see the day they finish this blasted railroad!"

"Who you hauling for?" Keegan asked.

"Old Penrose Capps!" The teamster pronounced the name like an oath, then described Capps and the country in general with genuine profanity. His sharp Adam's apple fascinated Keegan as it shot up and down between the ridged cords of the teamster's wrinkled throat.

"I was figuring on going to work here for someone," Keegan laughed. "Maybe I better pass up Capps."

"A hard nut!" The teamster spat. "If he can't make it on his work estimates he takes it out of the cooking pot." He wagged his head.

"He's a rustler, harder than a woman's heart. There's two things he likes: to see how much a horse can pull and how much a man can lift."

"How's Keegan's outfit to work for?" Reno asked.

"Pretty good when old Liash was around. He got himself shot up taking in a payroll   died a day or two ago, I hear, and now the layout's falling to pieces." The teamster shook his head. "Old Liash Keegan wasn't the pickhandle type, but at that he was tougher than Capps. Even so, he didn't try to starve a man to death.

"It's a mean country. They don't need no railroad out here. What we should've had was signs every ten feet along the Mississippi saying, 'Stay home, you fool!' "

Keegan grinned, thinking that it would

take more than a good team of horses to drag this weathered old veteran out of the country. The man would still be cursing and making dire predictions the day the railroad was finished.

After receiving thanks for his aid and a drink of skull-lifting whisky from a flat bottle, Keegan led his team back down the hill to pick up his wagon.

He passed the tank wagon before long and began to near the biggest construction camp he'd seen so far. That would be Penrose Capps' outfit, according to the girl's description.

Where the road ran close to grade a-building a man waved Keegan to stop and yelled of an impending blast in a narrow lava cut. The gray team jumped and trembled when dynamite ripped against the rock, sending dust and fragments into the hot air.

Shallow holes, Keegan estimated by the sound — and not pulling ground very well. He noticed that no one waited for a powderman to check for missed shots. Pushers sent scrapermen and pick and shovel workers swarming into the cut while it was yet obscured by dust and smoke.

Keegan left his rig near a trampled place on the outskirts of camp where a few lame horses were shaking off flies and foraging for bits of hay. He walked toward a wooden water tank where a small keg was catching a leak.

Stacks of tools before a brown-topped tent with a scalloped overhang and the sounds of hammer and anvil from within told Keegan the nature of at least one of the twenty-five or thirty large tents that comprised the camp.

He shooed flies, then lifted the keg in both hands and tilted it to drink. Looking over the rim, he saw a burly, slope-shouldered man emerge from the blacksmith's shop and come stumping toward him.

The man wore a greasy black Scotch cap pushed back on a bullet head that was bald and freckled as far as exposed. He wasn't tall, but he was round and thick and appeared to weigh as much if not more than Keegan. In spite of his somewhat shambling walk the fellow came in a purposeful straight line — right at Keegan, who lowered the keg to catch his breath.

The man stopped before Keegan and gave him a careful appraisal from small bloodshot eyes. He stood as if waiting for Keegan to speak.

Keegan tipped the keg and drank again. The other man dipped a broad thumb and bent forefinger into a pouch and loaded the inside of his under lip with an enormous cargo of snuff.

His voice was a low growl, his words barely audible when he said, "You got time to get in a few hours today."

Keegan set the keg down. "You the boss?"

"I'm Penrose Capps. I said you got time to get that team on a wheeler and go to work."

Keegan studied the contractor. Capps was wearing a pair of loopless pants that were too big. Excess material had been bunched together in front to form dusty pleats that overhung a worn brown belt. Capps' face was round and meaty, his green eyes steady as they rested on Keegan and plainly said that drinking water was a sinful waste of time when a man could be out separating his ribs from his backbone in honest toil.

"I'm not looking for work here," Keegan said.

Capps' little eyes glinted as if he had been insulted — and disobeyed. "Oregon boomer?" His disgust was evident.

"Headed for Keegan's outfit." Keegan reached into the keg and removed two swimming flies, wondering if two were all there had been before he drank.

Capps grunted, glancing at the water keg as if the act of removing flies were a sign of feminine delicacy. "Keegan, huh? That water costs me a fortune."

"What's the matter with Keegan's outfit? You sound like they did you wrong."

"Stay clear of that layout," Capps said.

"Are you warning me or advising me?"

Capps sucked at the bulge under his lower lip. "Take it either way." He looked over at the gray team. "You got time to get in part of a shift, boomer."

Keegan started for his wagon. "Thanks for the drink."

Capps glowered like an angry bear. "Try feeding your team on that — and see how fat they get."

"I'll bring you a canteen of lukewarm water with two flies in it the next time I'm by," Keegan said.

"On your way back from Oregon, huh?" Capps turned and lumbered back toward the blacksmith's shop. Violent hammering began as soon as he set his course.

Keegan saw his father's camp approximately a mile farther west along the sun-yellowed line of slope stakes. About three fourths of the way to it, near a camel-backed hill that seemed to sit dead in the way of the survey, he saw a smaller group of tents on the desolate lava rock.

When he reached them he stopped and looked around. Three of the tents were approximately eighteen by thirty feet and sat in a row; behind them several smaller shelters were set haphazardly. Keegan eyed a stack of empty whisky barrels and guessed the nature of this establishment.

He got down and went over to the middle one of the three largest structures. Stale heat and the acrid smell of warm whisky enveloped him when he stepped inside. Half asleep, with his elbows propped on a wooden bar that ran almost across the far end of the tent, a bald-headed bartender rested with the palms of his hands pushing his jowls.

The place swarmed with sluggish flies that appeared to be as stupid with heat as the dozing bartender.

There were three poker tables, two of them in use by ten men who gave Keegan no more than casual glances as he walked toward the bar. Two of the players, by their dress and hands, were obviously housemen, Keegan decided. The others looked like any of the hundreds of construction workers he had passed on this trip.

Yawning and stroking downward on his

cheeks, the bartender came half awake, his cheek-pulling exposing remarkably blood-shot underlids. He picked up a dirty whisky glass, shook it, and filled it from one of the four barrels sitting behind the bar, two on each side of opened flaps through which no air seemed to come.

The bartender set the glass before Keegan and watched him without interest. "Hot, ain't it?"

Keegan admitted that it was hot, and the bartender began to lapse into another doze.

Glancing toward the nearest table, Keegan met the gaze of a brown-faced player who was studying him openly. Though the man's forehead was neither sloping nor low, a huge, projecting nose and a pointed, thrusting jaw gave his whole head a jutting effect as if he were pushing his face forward belligerently.

Suddenly the fellow yawned. In the middle of it someone grunted at him to ante. He blinked and went back to the game, and Keegan found himself yawning from the two recent examples he had seen.

Someone momentarily blocked sunshine from flooding debris on the rock and dirt floor near the front of the tent. The bartender came wide awake in two blinks, without benefit of cheek-rubbing or yawning.

The man standing just inside the tent was six feet two or three, stripped to the waist and deeply tanned on every inch of a wide-shouldered, deep-chested torso. In odd contrast his face was pale beneath coal-black hair. His boots were unusually small in proportion to the rest of his size. His pearl-gray trousers, held up by a wide black belt, were trim about his hips, emphasizing his tapering build.

He came slowly down the room, raising his arms high, then doubling them against his chest in a luxurious stretching of muscles. Like a mountain lion, Keegan thought.

Several of the poker players called him "Carson." The bartender was more polite in his greeting. "Pretty hot in the tent, Mr. Albo?"

Keegan saw that Albo's brown chest was covered with fine perspiration drops. "Never could sleep in the daytime — more than two hours." Albo's smile was easy and friendly.

The bartender set a bottle on the bar and produced two clean glasses wrapped in white cloth. Albo turned jet-black eyes on Keegan and studied him with frank curiosity. "Oregon, friend?"

Keegan shook his head. "Doesn't anybody ever stop to work?"

Albo smiled. "Those with sound sense go right on out of this desert. You appear to have good sense."

"I'm stopping." Keegan nodded toward his father's camp. "There."

"Oh?" Albo glanced at Keegan's glass. "Drink?"

Keegan nodded and finished the barrel whisky. The bartender pushed one of the clean glasses toward him.

Over their filled glasses Albo and Keegan weighed each other. "You wouldn't be figuring on pulling that outfit out of its hole, would you?" Albo asked.

Someone grumbling about bad luck at the nearest poker table hesitated for just a tick before resuming his complaint. Keegan glanced toward the table and saw that it was the brown-faced man who was talking.

Now that Albo's words were gone forever, Keegan tried to recall the tone, searching for a hint of challenge. He looked squarely into the pale face and said quietly, "I might be figuring on that. Why?"

Albo's eyes narrowed a little at the harshness in Keegan's voice, but he spoke carelessly. "An idle question, friend. They could use a strong hand in that camp, I hear." Albo's eyes were steady. "You strike me as having that sort of look about you."

"Thanks." Keegan bought the drinks.

While Albo was pouring his own Keegan looked back at the poker table and saw the brown-faced man studying him quietly. One of the players cursed the fellow's inattention and told him it was his deal.

—CHAPTER FIVE—

As Keegan drove on toward what he was already calling in his own mind his camp he reflected that the gambling and whisky tents he had just left might create some problems he would have to deal with.

Whisky and gambling clung to construction like evil brothers that were hard to shake off. In this case the parasites were altogether too close, even if they were on government land with a government license pinned on the canvas wall behind the bar.

Keegan observed his first trouble when he reached the nearest grading crew. Men were swinging sledges against a huge mass of lava rock thrown up by a blast in a shallow cut. Scraper teams and dump carts were standing by idly waiting for cargo that would be long in forthcoming.

If Laraine Grieve had warned of his coming Keegan saw no sign of it among the men. He left the wagon and went over to where a man who now and then yelled an order was sitting glumly on a bag of oats near the teams.

The foreman glanced with no more than average interest at Keegan. "If you're looking for work you'll have to see Stroud."

"Who's he?" Keegan asked.

"The super."

Keegan tucked the name away. "How come you're using black powder?"

"Because that's all we got." The foreman cursed. "Look at the size of that chunk!"

"Can't you get dynamite?"

"Sure! We'll have some in a few days. We ran out just about the time Capps stole a load from us." He glared toward the distant Capps camp.

"Stole it?" Keegan asked.

"He says the teamster brought it into his camp by mistake. Well, we know Capps was about out of dynamite too, so he just bulldozed our load away from the teamster. Oh, he'll pay for it when he gets around to it, but in the meantime —" the foreman gestured toward a hammerman who was pausing to wipe sweat off his forehead with his arm — "we're tearing up chunks ten horses couldn't budge."

One of the teamsters cursed Capps and said, "I'd like to've seen him try that when old Liash was here!"

"Where will I most likely find Stroud?" Keegan asked.

The foreman jerked his hand as if too tired or disgusted to speak, indicating the general direction of camp.

"On the west end of the work," one of the teamsters said. He glanced with approval at the well matched pair of gray horses hitched to the wagon. "Seems like I ought to know that mule."

On the edge of camp Keegan watered his animals in a trough beneath a wooden tank, doling out warm water through a length of fire hose fitted to the tank. He drove over to where baled hay was tumbled in a disorderly pile on the ground.

Nearby he saw the team of black geldings Laraine Grieve had driven that day, picketed just out of reach of the hay. He unharnessed the grays and turned them loose, then saddled Bear Trap and started a tour.

The tents had been new not long before, he noticed. They were well set up but his years of army training rebelled against the debris that had been allowed to pile up around the camp. Tin cans almost blocked the rear entrance to the cook tent; scrapers, wheels, tools that needed sharpening were scattered here and there.

He saw two men lounging against the shady side of a bunk tent, half asleep as they fumbled with harness they evidently were supposed to be repairing. He dismounted before one of the bunk tents and looked inside to see three men lying on their cots, obviously sleeping off hangovers.

Dull picks and broken tools were lying in front of a blacksmith's shop, and no sounds were coming from the anvil.

He rode down the survey line where crews were scattered along the work. Few paid him more than passing attention, and everybody seemed infected with the same listlessness that had characterized the first group he'd watched. He talked to three foremen who evinced the resigned disgust that runs like an epidemic through an organization when a job begins to go sour.

This job was very sour, Keegan thought angrily.

"Buck Stroud?" said a wide, black-jowled teamster. "He's over there with that last bunch." He pointed to where a dozen or more teams were pulling scrapers along the edges of the grade.

Keegan took the gun from his belt and tied it on the saddle as he rode away. He was sorry that he hadn't left it in the wagon, for he had no desire to give the impression of a swaggering gunman and had observed the keen looks some of the men had directed at the weapon.

He dismounted and walked toward a huge man who was directing scrapermen. Either because of nervousness or irritation, the fellow whirled quickly when Keegan walked up behind him and spoke his name.

Stroud wiped sweat off his forehead and pushed his dusty hat back. He was younger than Keegan, red-headed, with quick-moving green eyes above prominent cheek-bones. In spite of a three-days' growth of sandy beard there was something almost intangible in Stroud's looks that just for an instant reminded Keegan of his long-dead brother.

"We ain't hiring right now," Stroud said. He started to turn away.

"This is the first camp where somebody didn't try to hire me," Keegan said.

One of the scrapermen, the lines from his team looped around his neck, sat down and started to remove a boot.

Stroud swung back to Keegan, who wondered whether the big superintendent was naturally short-tempered or whether the job was working on him. "You heard me!" Stroud said.

Keegan gave him the benefit of the doubt: the job was enough, in its present state, to make any man quarrelsome.

The teamster removing his boot looked at Keegan insolently. "Why don't you go back to one of those other camps?" The speaker's meaty, black-stubbled cheeks puffed out as he hawked dust from his throat and spat.

He was a squat man, almost as large around as Capps. Nature had given him plenty of room for features and then had scrambled them in a bunch smack in the center of his face — close-set eyes, small nose knit tightly to the skull, and a tight mouth that twisted when he spoke.

"I figured maybe they wouldn't let a man sit down to take imaginary rocks out of a knee-high boot," Keegan told the teamster. Then he looked at Stroud, whose eyes had gone hard suddenly. "Would you come over by the mule, Stroud? I'd like to talk to you."

"Talk right here!" Stroud said.

His anger, Keegan realized, had sprung from the implication that he had overlooked or been fooled by the teamster stalling with his boot.

"This is private," Keegan said.

The teamster laughed shortly. "He wants to borrow money, Buck."

"Shut up, Derwent!" Stroud spoke

without taking his eyes from Keegan. His face showed indecision and impatience.

Keegan decided that Stroud had been harassed by his duties until he was as edgy as a shedding rattler.

"Talk right here," Stroud said.

Keegan introduced himself. He saw Stroud's face relax a little and heard the teamsters within hearing stop their work.

"The fair-haired boy the Old Man was always talking about," Derwent said. "He don't like the way you're running the job, Buck."

Stroud tensed again. "What's the matter with the way I'm running things?"

"You let him —" Keegan nodded toward Derwent, who was on his feet now — "put questions in your head?"

The superintendent's face darkened. "Nobody puts questions in my head! What's the matter with the way things are running?"

Keegan eyed him quietly. "Whatever your real troubles are — this whole job is a mess from start to go. I wanted to talk to you reasonably without any loud-mouthed interference, but since you asked for it — that's the way she stacks!"

Stroud's eyes seemed to turn deeper green. His face went white and he stepped closer to Keegan. "What do you figure on doing about it?"

Regretfully Keegan saw that there was no peaceful way out without losing the respect of the whole camp before he even got started. Stroud's own touchy temper and the loudmouthed Derwent had forced the issue.

"Fire you — to start," Keegan said quietly.

Stroud's smile was a wicked grimace. "It's easy to say. It's easy to put on the timebooks, but —" His smile went into a snarl.

"Whatever you want." Keegan tried to step back fast to get room for his long arms.

He blocked the blow that came at his chest by taking it on his elbow. His elbow was driven back against his ribs so hard that he was knocked down as cleanly as if the power had come directly. He caught himself with his hands as his body struck the ground.

Stroud made no move to use his boots. He stood waiting, grinning in pure joy.

Keegan got up, knowing that if he stopped one or two more punches like that he would be boss in name only around this camp. He slid his right foot forward, then shifted the other one ahead quickly and jabbed Stroud in the mouth.

Then Keegan let his right go, straight and hard. It was a touch high. It cracked against the corner of Stroud's wide mouth and blotched one cheekbone. Blood began to spread down the superintendent's jaw.

He beat aside Keegan's next two tries and moved forward.

"In the guts, Stroud!" Derwent yelled. "That first one almost got him!"

Keegan rocked Stroud's head with another jab. The redhead grinned. He caught Keegan's wrist on the next attempt and jerked him forward.

Sunlight seemed to lose its force. The day turned gray for Keegan and he thought his heart had stopped beating from the shock of the blow just above it. His knees seemed numb and useless. He hooked one arm around Stroud's sweaty neck and held on.

"Knee him, Stroud!" Derwent's voice seemed to come to Keegan from a long distance.

Instinctively Keegan swung sidewise, but the superintendent didn't bring up his knee. Instead he was chopping sidewise with his right hand at Keegan's head buried against his shoulder. He may have known that the skull of man is quite hard, but Stroud was panting in rage. He kept trying.

Keegan let his weight sag and held on. Over Stroud's shoulder the figures of silent teamsters began to quit weaving and assume almost normal form as Keegan felt some of his strength coming back.

He could distinguish features of the watching men when Stroud gave up his ineffective head pounding and tried to force Keegan away. Keegan helped him. He let his body sag a little lower, then thrust his shoulder up as hard as he could under Stroud's jaw.

The impact was solid. Stroud grunted. Keegan's shoulder signaled that it was splintered, at least, but he managed to break free and step back.

And then he stepped in and caught Stroud just below the breastbone. It was a blow to reduce steam in any man. Stroud's mouth came wide open and he gasped. Keegan measured him for another of the same. And then Keegan found himself sitting on the ground once more, his back teeth aching from a straight blow that had landed squarely in the middle of his forehead.

He got up and walked in. He had to. He knew that in a few moments if he didn't get lucky he was going to fall flat on his face from the pain in his heart. He nailed Stroud with another straight right below the joining of the ribs. He straightened him with a leaping uppercut that made Keegan's sore shoulder wince.

And then, less than an arm's length away, Keegan put all he had left into a simon-pure round-house that cracked against the angle of Stroud's jaw.

The red-head went down. He rolled on his stomach, got on his knees — and while Keegan prayed for strength enough to stay on his own feet — Stroud slumped back to earth.

Keegan's legs dragged when he tried to turn briskly. He looked toward Derwent, whose face was no more than a big hazy blot above a dark outline.

"Get back to work!" Keegan said. His voice didn't sound quite natural, but he saw the blot begin to move. Chains began to jangle, hooves sounded against the rocks, and scrapers began their grating sound.

—CHAPTER SIX—

Keegan walked to the mule. He didn't trust himself to try to mount, so he grasped the reins near the bit and let his hand slide until he felt the knot in the end of the leather.

He led the mule away, walking slowly toward a small rise to the west. As if from a great distance he heard someone laugh and say, "You can tell he's Liash's boy all right enough!"

Behind the little hill, which was scarcely high enough to hide Bear Trap, Keegan lay down against the slope. He lay there until his vision was clear and his legs began to feel normal, but he couldn't lose the dull headache at the base of his brain or the soreness in his chest.

He rode slowly back along the grade. Stroud was gone. The scrapermen were working steadily, including Derwent, who looked at Keegan as casually as if he were an old acquaintance.

Keegan watched the work without speaking. He glanced back at the apparently finished grade he had just passed and then at the shallow excavation before him. Scrapermen were making almost futile efforts to find enough material along the sides to fill the long cut.

He waited until Derwent made a turn near the mule.

"Why do we have to backfill this?" Keegan asked.

Derwent stopped his team. He swiped a dirty sleeve across his forehead and put one foot on the bottom of the overturned scraper. "Specifications. They say rolling stock can't stand a beating from track laid smack on this busted rock. So we have to go a foot or so below grade and backfill with whatever we can find."

Backfill material was scarce, little patches of wind-blown earth or sand here and there in shallow rock pockets.

"It would be a darned sight easier to put a string of gandydancers on both sides to throw in by hand what they could find — and haul the rest in dump carts from wherever we could scrape it up," Derwent said.

Keegan considered the suggestion. It took no more than a glance to see that scrapers were not moving enough backfill to warrant the wear and tear on men, teams and tools.

Derwent grinned, his mouth never completely relaxing its tight oval. "But you got plenty of scrapers and nothing to move — since we're out of stick powder."

Keegan studied the bottom of the shallow cut where backfill had not been dumped. The lava rock was not solid, but it was keyed together and lay in a jumbled mass without definite cleavage. Shattering was the only method of getting results in that formation.

He'd do something as soon as possible about Capps and that load of diverted dynamite, he vowed.

Keegan studied Derwent. The man certainly was an ugly brute with a snarly disposition. There was nothing about him that Keegan found to his liking as far as physical appearance went. Still, the man had talked sense. The suggestion he had made about backfilling was simple enough — once it was made.

Unlike an ordinary teamster, Derwent had known why the grade had to be backfilled. Keegan was not foolish enough to think he could run the job; he knew something about construction, considerable about rock work, but he suspected Derwent knew a great deal more about the job over all.

"You want Stroud's place?" he asked. "Same pay, starting from noon today?"

Nothing showed in Derwent's eyes. "If I can run the job my way."

"We'll argue about that if we have reason to later on," Keegan said. "You run it your way as long as it fits my ideas about getting the work done."

Derwent nodded.

Keegan rode away thinking that there was more than a suggestion of deep-seated meanness about Derwent; that he didn't trust the man by any means. But if he could get the work done . . .

He heard loud voices from the blacksmith's shop as he neared camp. Dismounting near the wide entrance, Keegan went inside.

A lean man in leather apron was standing at the anvil, tapping the pritchett hole with a cathead hammer as he looked with brooding, deep-set eyes at a chunky man waving his arms and pointing at a pile of dull picks near the door.

"The points bust or they mush up! For three days now we been having trouble with every pick you sharpen!"

Keegan recognized the chunky man as the foreman he had seen sitting glumly on the sack of oats a short time before.

Grimed with soot from countless fires,

the smith's face was as dark as his brooding eyes. He was a muscular figure even as he stood quietly, the end of the hammer handle brushing up and down against his apron. His mop of dark hair showed wide gray streaks.

It struck Keegan that he had seen a pair of dark eyes almost like the blacksmith's a short time before; then he remembered — the girl, Laraine Grieve, had said her father was the blacksmith.

Grieve looked at the stocky foreman. "Get out," he said tonelessly. "I run this shop."

"You run it like a bankrupt! —"

"Get out!" Grieve said. He was no longer brooding: he was getting ready to explode. "Get out, or I'll pitch you out on your head!"

"The devil you will!" the foreman yelled.

He grabbed a heavy railroad pick. The handle was dry and there was no burlap in the eye. He raised the tool above his head, so high it pushed a bulge into the smoke-grimed canvas.

Keegan reached out to grab the pick.

He didn't have to. The heavy metal slid down the handle and struck the holder solidly on the head. He dropped without a sound.

"Any fool ought to know better than to raise a pick with a dried-out handle," Grieve said. He laid the hammer on the anvil block. "Give me a hand."

They carried the unconscious foreman outside and stretched him along the shady side of the tent.

"I'd throw water on him — only it's scarce," Grieve said. He seemed to see Keegan clearly for the first time. "Who're you?"

Keegan introduced himself. Grieve's somber eyes lighted a little, but his hand-shake was as loose as water-soaked hay. "You should've been here sooner. Liash is going to lose his hind end on this job."

"So I hear," Keegan said. "What's the matter with the picks?"

Grieve eyed him steadily a moment, then turned and walked back into the tent. "The coal's no good," he said. "Nothing you get out here is any good."

Keegan stood in the opening, watching the foreman, who was stirring a little. Then he glanced at the disorderly pile of dull tools inside and outside the shop. "Looks like you need a helper."

"I've run the shop on bigger jobs than this without no helper."

Keegan nodded. Along with cooks and

timekeepers, blacksmiths were the most touchy men on any job of this kind. But this was no time to bow to temperament. "Tomorrow," Keegan said, "you'll have a helper. Pick him yourself, or I will."

The foreman grunted a little and sat up, brushing one hand against the tent wall, feeling the top of his head with the other. He saw Keegan and glared at him. "You hit me!" he accused Reno.

"You knocked yourself stem-winding by letting a pick slide down the handle," Keegan said. He grinned. "You've had worse jolts than that from a shot of bad whisky."

Comprehension broke in the foreman's eyes. He felt his head with both hands.

"Get up and go take care of your men," Keegan said. "There'll be picks tomorrow if we have to work all night." He looked at Grieve. "Get your helper and put that steel in shape."

Keegan walked toward the bunk tent where he had seen the three men sleeping. He heard the stocky foreman, all his belligerence jarred out of him, ask Grieve, "Who let that crusty cuss loose around here?"

Grieve's deep voice rumbled something. When Keegan looked back from the front of the tent the foreman was hurrying off to his work, still feeling his head with one hand.

The bunk tent was filled with heat, the sour odor of whisky, and the blast of unclean blankets. One of the drunks was sitting on the edge of his cot, staring at the dirt floor as if waiting for relieving death.

Keegan spilled the other two out of their beds and kicked them into consciousness. They staggered to their feet and blinked at him in bewilderment that rapidly began to change to rage.

"Get out and finish your shift — or head for the time shack," Keegan ordered. "If you've got to get loaded in the daytime, sleep on the floor of the dump where you get the whisky!"

The sitter shook his head and grinned. "It's too hard on Albo's floors." He stood up, fell backward on his cot, made it to his feet once more and blinked at an unfamiliar world. "Work'll kill me, but I'm going to try it. I'll be better off dead anyway."

The other two looked at Keegan and then at each other. "The devil with this job," one said. His companion nodded.

"Get your money," Keegan said.

They began to roll their blankets. "They don't owe me much," one sneered. "But it'll probably bust this Joe McGee outfit."

Keegan walked out, hoping among other things that there was enough money on hand to pay the pair, and a few others there might be later.

One of the men inside the tent had a sudden functioning of the brain. "Who was that anyway?" he asked in a deeply puzzled tone.

"I don't aim to find out," his companion said.

As Keegan headed for the mess tent he saw the man who had said he'd try work drinking from a pail of the water tank. The fellow saw Keegan, took another big gulp of water, and went zigzagging toward the nearest crew.

Once upon a time the wooden tables in the mess tent had been washed. Keegan frowned at the rows of tin plates, set close together and lined as if by transit. He started to pick one up but it didn't move. He leaned over and took a close look.

Under a film of grease and food fragments he saw three nails driven through the plate into the trestled plank beneath.

The cook shack was an extension of the long mess tent. An immensely fat man in a filthy flour sack apron was asleep in a chair near the rear entrance. A one-eyed man wearing a greasy black Stetson and a pimply youth in dirty overalls were cutting biscuit dough on a table where flies swarmed.

"Nothing till supper," the one-eyed man said wearily. "This ain't no short order house."

Keegan looked into a large copper wash boiler on the stove and wrinkled his nose at the odor rising from what must have been a stew.

He nodded toward the fat sleeper. "That the cook?"

Both helpers looked at Keegan's face and nodded rapidly.

Keegan took two long steps and kicked the chair from under the cook. The man seemed to catch himself in midair. He fell, but he was on his feet in an instant.

In deference to such agility and his own sore chest, Keegan picked up a meat cleaver and slapped it thoughtfully against his palm. "Clean up this place," he said. "Tear those plates off the table and put on ones that you can wash clean." He waved the cleaver toward the stove. "Don't cook another mess like that."

The cook looked at Keegan's eyes and at the cleaver. He glanced at his helpers and said nothing.

"If you need anything, including more help, let me know or tell McLean," Keegan said, wondering who the heck McLean was.

He turned and strode back through the mess tent. At the end of a table he grabbed a plate in both hands and wrenched it free, looking for a moment at slime that had seeped to the plank through the nail holes.

He stepped outside and spun the plate through the hot air, watching until it fell somewhere in the scraggly sage.

Then he noticed the two men who had been dozing over their harness mending a while before. They were working now. "Where's McLean?" Keegan asked.

"Commissary tent," one of the men said. He began to pick up rivets that had fallen between his legs.

—CHAPTER SEVEN—

"You're Reno Keegan, eh?"

Keegan nodded, studying the man behind the counter in the commissary, the only place in camp so far where order was apparent. "Core McLean?"

"Um-hmm." Iron gray hair as crisp as grass on a frosty morning bulged in one complete, tight whorl all over McLean's head. He was of medium height, compactly built. His nose was thin, jutting, and sunburned. He weighed Keegan as carefully as a man watching his poke on untrustworthy scales.

He shook hands with the air of a man reserving judgment while observing the amenities.

Keegan sat down on the edge of the counter.

"Get off the counter," McLean said. "This ain't no Indian trading post."

There was a whack of authority in McLean's voice that made Keegan obey without thinking.

"You've played merry hell so far,"

McLean said. "You fired the one man that might have got the work done. I hope *you* know something about running a grading crew." His tone implied that the hope was vain.

They weighed each other, Keegan deciding that McLean was much younger than his hair indicated. He held a quiet competency in his eyes, the look of a man who would accept neither violence nor bluff.

"I had no intention of firing Stroud," Keegan said. "His temper got away and —" He shrugged.

McLean said nothing. His eyes, Keegan thought, were the kind that cut through words and examine the thoughts behind them.

"Derwent has the job now," Keegan said.

"Bill Derwent!" McLean examined Keegan's face closely as if looking for evidences of idiocy missed in his initial scrutiny. "Come on back to my office and let's talk things over."

Keegan followed the storekeeper to the back end of the tent where a partition of baled hay separated the commissary from a little room that held a cot, a battered army field desk and two chairs. McLean gathered some newspapers from the cot, folded them carefully and put them on the desk. He waved Keegan toward a chair and sat down on the cot.

"You don't like Derwent?" Keegan asked.

McLean's gaze was steady. "No. He's worked as superintendent for some of the biggest outfits in the West, and he's always been fired as a trouble-maker. His reputation for getting work done is good. Capps was the last one to let him go — and when Penrose Capps thinks a man is too rough to have around —" McLean shook his head.

"The work is why the outfit is here," Keegan said. "Stroud wasn't delivering."

"That's right. Stroud was a good man when your father was right behind him, but when Buck was left on his own he just wasn't quite the man to handle everything, hard as he worked. He was a hard worker." That, McLean plainly indicated, was a prime virtue in any man.

McLean hesitated for a while, staring at Keegan thoughtfully. "I'll tell you one reason why Liash nursed Stroud along: he reminded your father of your brother. Not that Buck wouldn't have made the riffle in time, mind you."

Keegan spoke quickly to cover old

thoughts that still hurt. "It's done now. We'll get along with Derwent — as long as he stays in line. Besides what little I've seen so far — what's the matter with this job?"

"It's been murder from the word go," McLean said quietly. "First off, Liash misjudged this rock — like every other contractor, including Capps. It looked loose and they thought it would move almost as easy as the sandy loam on the plains.

"Then Liash found out different. He had Grieve spend a week building two heavy, special ploughs to rip with. A handler got too deep, twisted one of them, and busted it before it did a morning's work. The next day Liash discovered that someone had used a sledge to ruin the other one during the night." McLean shrugged. "The plows didn't work anyway.

"One night somebody cut the hose from the water tank and drained several hundred dollars worth of water. That shut us down for two days while we were waiting for tank wagons to make that long haul. Half the camp got drunk at Albo's, and those that came back weren't fit to work for two days."

Keegan's mind leaped to the pale-faced, pleasant saloonkeeper who might or might not have been warning Keegan to stay away from this job.

"The hay burned one night," McLean said. "That caused the horses and mules — there's only a few spooky ones we have to picket — to scatter from hell to break-fast." McLean's face turned red with anger. "Hay costs us, laid down in camp, a hundred dollars a ton."

He held up two fingers. "For every dollar we spend for supplies we spend two getting them delivered here. You can see what a loss out here does to the camp. Liash put a guard at the tank and one on the horses, but somebody slipped into a storage tent behind the cook shack one night and threw kerosene on several hundred dollars worth of food — flour, bacon, saltside, rice —" McLean cursed bitterly.

"Go on," Keegan said.

"There were a dozen more things like that — tools smashcd up, filth thrown in the water tank one night when the guard went to sleep — dirty, underhanded things. Liash was having a bad enough time with the work, so he sent for you." McLean raised one hand. "It wasn't just that he was yelling for help. He'd been talking for several months of making up with you."

"Who knew I was coming?" Keegan asked.

McLean looked at the red bump raised on Keegan's forehead by Stroud's blow. "Everybody in camp, everybody between here and Yankee Falls. Liash was right proud of what he'd done."

"Still," Keegan said slowly, "nobody could be sure I was coming, even if they knew my father had written —"

"When Liash got through talking you were as good as here."

Keegan nodded, slowly recalling almost forgotten habits of his father. "Have you any idea who shot my father?" he asked.

McLean shook his head. "He and Stroud and I were bringing in a payroll when three or maybe four men tackled us just this side of Coyote Hill. Stroud, we know for sure, wounded one. We stood 'em off and got clear, but they shot Liash twice, once in the side and once in the chest."

"You think they could have been some of the same men who have been raising ructions in the camp?" Keegan asked.

"Maybe. Half the camp was over at Albo's that night, so there's no way of proving who might have slipped away. When a contractor rides toward a bank along about payday, there's plenty of toughs just a-waiting. One gang nicked Capps for about twenty thousand."

McLean lowered his voice to a whisper. "It was a double payroll we were bringing in, and a little more for current expenses — all Liash had left." He looked at the hay partition significantly. "We've met one payday. The rest of the money —"

Baled hay, Keegan thought, was not a very good place in which to conceal the company's resources, but he could think of no better place.

McLean seemed to read his thoughts. "It's better to have it on hand than be taking a chance on a holdup every time you go after it," he said.

There was logic in that, Keegan thought. He watched the ceaseless probing and thrusting of McLean's eyes, and recalled Liash Keegan's statement that the storekeeper was a man to trust. Liash certainly had backed up his belief by leaving his money in McLean's care.

Reno Keegan could do no less than trust McLean also.

Briefly he told the storekeeper about Walker's death, inquiring at the end, "Was anyone missing from camp yesterday?"

McLean shook his head. "The timebook — I'm the timekeeper too — was full except for two men sleeping off drunks. The only person who was that far out of this camp was Laraine Grieve, the blacksmith's girl."

"I met her," Keegan said. "What did *she* go to town after?"

McLean obviously considered the question trifling. "She has friends there she visits. Besides, we needed some fresh beef and canned goods a little quicker than the freighters could haul it."

McLean's eyes didn't leave Keegan's face. "If your friend *was* shot because someone thought he was you — you wouldn't expect the killer to make himself conspicuous by being gone from camp two or three days, would you?"

"I just wanted to be sure," Keegan said. "The way it stacks to me right now, we've got at least one man here in camp trying to wreck things and at least one working with him on the outside, maybe at Albo's or with Capps."

McLean's gaze was hard and steady. "Or some of the other construction camps or the track-layer's camp — or even hanging out in the hills with the hunting crews."

"Hunting crews?"

"The meat hunters that sell venison saddles for three cents a pound," McLean said. "Back in the mountains there's three or four camps of them."

"We'll stick to finding the man right here

in camp," Keegan said. He watched McLean's face closely. "Any ideas?"

McLean shook his head. "I've considered everybody at one time or another, including Grieve. Him and your father were partners several years ago in Nebraska and they made a pretty good-sized pile on three jobs. Grieve wanted to pull out right then and buy the farm he's been talking about for years, but Liash talked him into one more job, a spur contract in Colorado."

McLean shrugged. "By the time they got everything paid off there wasn't a piece of equipment left or a horse to ride out of camp. Your father, Grieve and I walked into Denver flat broke. Liash didn't take it hard. Right away he went to borrowing and figuring how to get started up again.

"But Grieve — I thought for a while he was going to shoot himself. Liash tried to get him to stick with the partnership and try again, but Grieve was cured of the operating end. He said he'd stick to black-smithing from then on. In a year Liash was making money again."

McLean waited for this information to soak in. "You see what I'm getting at?"

"You think he might have become bitter and jealous because his own lack of courage made him miss a good deal?"

"That's right," McLean said briskly. "On top of that he's brooding himself into something mean over Albo and Laraine." McLean raised one brow. "You mentioned Albo a minute ago. How — ?"

"I happened to bump into him," Keegan said.

McLean seemed to approve. "You've been getting around at that, haven't you?" He hesitated. "But there were too many holes in my theory about Grieve. Twice when things went haywire around here I happened to be right with him, so I know he didn't cause trouble *those* two times. Then another thing: he hasn't got the money to take over."

"Your idea is then," Keegan said slowly, "that someone wants to wreck the outfit so it'll be easy to pick up cheap. But the way these jobs out here look to me, who the devil would want a construction outfit?"

McLean didn't smile, and Keegan wondered if he ever had.

"The contractors that survive this stretch are going to move on toward Boise the next jump," McLean said. "Up there the ground is a whole lot different. Liash looked it over. He said it was money-making ground for sure, none of this mean rock. Capps figures on getting well up there, too."

From what Keegan knew of contractors they all figured on getting well on the next job when the immediate one began to lose money. They were no different from prospectors looking for sudden fortune on the next round.

McLean used his forefinger to emphasize his words. "Capps has been buying up equipment from contractors that went busted right along. Now if *this* outfit went broke and someone had the money to take it over, he could be like Capps and the rest — figuring on making a potful of money farther west.

"I mentioned Grieve, but I've suspected everybody else that had sense enough to run a job, including Stroud himself." McLean shook his head. "None of them fit. Not one has the money, even if they figured they could mcct thcir first payroll by moving enough yardage on a new job."

"How about Capps?" Keegan asked.

"Capps would take the food out of your mouth if he needed it or wanted it bad enough, but he wouldn't be sneaky and underhanded about doing it."

"He was pretty underhanded on that load of dynamite he grabbed," Keegan scowled.

"That's different," McLean said. "Liash

would've done the same thing to him if he could. In this game it's grab what you can and hold it if you're big enough. Capps will pay for the powder — or replace it."

"That won't replace the time and money we lost because we didn't have the dynamite when we needed it," Keegan said.

He looked past McLean and stared at the canvas wall. One of his next moves, he decided, would be an accounting with Penrose Capps over that diverted dynamite.

"No, I'm sure Capps isn't backing anybody to ruin this organization," McLean said. "From what I gather he's spread out just about as big as he can stand. Whoever is giving us trouble here —"

Boots crunched outside the commissary entrance and a man cursed sullenly. McLean stood up and peered over the top of the hay partition. He reached under the pillow on his cot, lifted a double-barreled derringer, and dropped it into his coat pocket as he moved toward the commissary.

Moving behind McLean and looking over his shoulder, Keegan went between the wall and the ends of the bales.

Two men had entered the commissary. One was standing near the entrance, holding a revolver. One eye was bloody and closed; his lips were puffed, his cheekbone gashed, and a patch of scalp was hanging over one ear.

The other man was leaning across the counter, reaching under it. He came up with a rifle and turned toward McLean and Keegan. His nose had been smashed sidewise and there was dust and dried blood all over his face.

Keegan felt for his gun and remembered that it was tied on the McClellan saddle outside on Bear Trap.

—CHAPTER EIGHT—

McLean went forward slowly, one hand in the pocket that held the derringer. He went around the end of the counter and kept going. Keegan went down the other side of the counter, matching McLean's pace.

"Watch that skinny one!" The man with the rifle held it stomach-high toward McLean. "We want our money — all of it!"

It came to Keegan then: the two had been fired, beaten in the process, and now were after no more than their wages. McLean must indeed have a hard reputation concerning paying off.

Keegan stopped a few paces away from the man with the revolver. The fellow didn't seem as confident as his companion, but the gun was cocked and he had one good eye.

"You'll get your money," Keegan said. "What happened?"

"Derwent!" The man with the handgun spat the name like an oath. "He started in on Mike. I jumped in to help Mike —"

"Derwent had a pick handle!" Mike said,

not taking his eyes from McLean, who stood calmly with one hand still in his coat pocket.

"What was the trouble over?" Keegan asked.

Mike held the rifle steady on McLean. "Derwent said I wasn't running my gang right."

Accuracy in that matter would be hard to establish, Keegan thought. He had hired Derwent to run the crews and was obliged to back him up, but not to approve brutality. However, these two were finished now. To keep them around camp would invite more trouble.

He looked at McLean, startled a little by the unwavering coldness of the store-keeper's eyes. "How have these men been on the job?"

"Good workers," McLean said without moving his gaze from Mike.

Keegan wondered if Mike realized how close to death he was.

The second man had lowered his revolver. In spite of his battered features his face showed that he hadn't had his heart in the affair in the first place. And now Keegan's calmness was disarming him.

"Are we buying deer meat from anybody?" Keegan asked the storekeeper.

McLean watched Mike. "No."

Keegan spoke to the two beaten men. "If you want your money you can have it. If you want to hunt deer for the camp I'll furnish a team and a wagon and pay you three cents a pound for all the haunches you bring in."

Mike lowered the rifle slowly, turning to look at his companion.

"You got only a few days coming," McLean said.

The two battered men looked at each other and then at Keegan. Five minutes later the details were settled. The pair would get the quoted price per pound; McLean was to let them draw camp stores to be charged against their first delivery.

They left to seek the cook, who was the camp doctor in addition to his other duties.

McLean stood with his recovered rifle, looking thoughtfully at the shelves built against the tent wall. Finally he laid the gun behind a stack of shirts and trousers. "Too many men know where I've been keeping that," he said as though talking to himself.

"Do you always pay off around here with a gun in your hands?" Keegan asked.

"We pay nothing less than half-shifts," McLean said. "Sometimes there's arguments

— and these men are tough."

Keegan remembered Capps' remarks about getting in a few hours' work that afternoon. "How about Capps?"

"He pays nothing less than full shifts," McLean said.

Contracting, Keegan decided, might be just a bit tougher than mining.

"You *might* get your team and wagon back," McLean said. "Mike was a good foreman. Pretty honest too."

McLean's eyes had already told Keegan the answer to his next question, but he asked it anyway. "Suppose those two had insisted on a full shift's pay?"

McLean looked mildly surprised. "There's two forty-one slugs in this Remington. When men are holding guns on you they're asking for trouble, and the law can't have any comeback — if there was any law."

Derwent might be tough with a pick handle, Keegan thought, but deep and solid in McLean was a cold-bloodedness that went deeper than toughness, because no part of it was assumed.

"We'd better go over the books," McLean said.

"After I see Derwent."

Keegan observed a definite change as he rode past the grading crews. No foreman was sitting now; the men were working a little harder. They sized him up without speaking and he knew that everything he had done so far had spread to every man.

That Derwent had not had a walkaway with the two men he'd just fired was evident when Keegan found the burly superintendent near a drilling crew. Derwent's face showed livid marks beneath the black stubble, and one ear had been torn.

He picked up two drills from a jackstraw pile of used steel and extended them toward Keegan. One was broken; the other had mushroomed before the tempering colors had worn away. "You got to do something about that," Derwent said.

His voice, Keegan thought, would never be anything but a snarl. "I will," Keegan said curtly. "I don't know what your trouble with Mike and that other fellow was about, but from now on do your firing without using a club. If you're not man enough to handle men with your hands — when you're forced to it — this job is deep enough for you right now."

Derwent stared savagely. "I can handle any man on this job!" His look included Keegan.

"Do it then. I want work — not bashed heads."

"Them that ask for trouble —" Derwent said.

"Will get it."

They looked at each other with complete understanding. Keegan rode back to the commissary and details he was afraid he would have trouble understanding. But McLean spoke clearly and his accounts were not hard to follow. He was proud of his records too.

"Maybe you know," he said, "that most contractors figure their work like this: they take a job, do it, and when it's over they count their money to see if they've got more or less than when they started."

Keegan grinned. "That's the acid test for sure."

McLean looked outraged.

Just before the end of the ten-hour shift Keegan came out of the commissary with a fairly complete grasp of the business end of the job, at least.

He didn't like what he'd found out. Liash had dropped forty thousand in this job so far; there was approximately twenty thousand in gold concealed in baled hay in McLean's quarters. Keegan had counted it and McLean had returned the canvas sacks to the hiding place.

Fourteen thousand would meet the next

payroll for the few less than three hundred men employed. The rest of the money, McLean said, would just about cover expenses for two months, with the final estimate of yardage moved netting enough to meet the last payroll — if the job was finished by then.

Keegan knew the best he could do was get the job done without losing the outfit. McLean's figures showed that as far as expecting to make money — there wasn't a chance. Tomorrow, Keegan thought, I'll check the work and try to verify that.

Steady sounds of hammering came from the blacksmith's tent. Keegan decided to let Grieve ride one more day and see if there was an improvement in his work. Whenever he thought of Grieve his mind automatically jumped to Laraine, and then to Albo.

Keegan tried to submerge the last thoughts and concentrate. He had a fearful mess to get straightened out.

He watched smoke coming from the cook tent. At least that crew hadn't quit, which was a more than minor victory, considering the uncertain natures of cooks.

Men and teams began to leave the grade. The horses, one hundred and six of them, were Liash Keegan's property. The Old

Man, according to McLean, was dead-set against the prevailing practice of hiring men and their teams at three dollars a day.

Either way you had to feed the horses, Keegan thought. And with freighting costs the way they were . . . a hundred dollars a ton for hay!

He looked across from the commissary where three brand-new elevating graders were, each a two-thousand-dollar rig that was utterly worthless on this job. Farther west in that almost mythical land where there was soil instead of lava rock, the graders might be money-makers.

But the outfit would never get farther west if this job didn't pan out; and then Liash Keegan, if he recovered from his wounds, would have to start again. Keegan wondered if cold-eyed Whisper Jim would remember to write.

Sounds in the blacksmith's shop ceased. Keegan watched Grieve emerge and walk toward two small tents at the extreme west end of camp, near the horse yard. Keegan wondered why the smith didn't wear a hat on his coarse mane of gray-streaked black hair.

He looked at the men nearing camp. On the whole they were as tough-looking a lot as he had ever seen, trail towns, Leadville, and Alder Gulch not excluded. According to McLean twenty-five or thirty of them changed their names on the payroll every month.

He was starting toward the water tank when someone called his name. He turned to see Laraine Grieve coming. The small squares of her blue and white gingham dress were sharp and clean against the drabness of the camp and the desolate flat around it.

Keegan grinned. "You look like a woman now, with that gandy's kerchief off your hair and some of the dust washed off your face."

The smile and look she gave him in return made him realize that she never would allow him to forget that she was a woman.

An unusually loud burst of profanity from teamsters watering their horses from the trough at the tank made him turn and scowl.

"Never mind," the girl said. "It's in one ear and out the other. I practically grew up in these camps or around a blacksmith's shop."

The longer he looked at her the more certain Keegan was that he was forming a dislike for Carson Albo. "This is a hard life for a woman." He thought instantly how trite his words must sound.

"You talk like my father," she said, her tone carrying the sharp edge of mockery. "Everybody out here thinks any woman under eighty either belongs in a dance hall or should be married and having children."

Keegan decided that he was not a competent judge of such matters. Over her shoulder he saw Grieve come from the small tent on the west end of camp and send water flashing from a tin washpan. Grieve saw Keegan and Laraine and stood watching. Even at the distance he exuded an air of brooding quietness.

Keegan watched as the smith turned slowly and walked into the tent. "If you grew up in a blacksmith's shop maybe you can tell me what's wrong with the tools?"

His glance flicked back to Laraine. She was watching him with a keen, speculative look. Then she looked away, glancing toward teamsters taking their horses toward the yard. "They haven't been tempered very good," she said. "Dad has been worried and careless."

"Worried about you?"

Her color didn't change. She gave him a cool look. "If that's any of your business — yes."

"The condition of the tools is my

business." As he looked at her the thought began to grow that perhaps he might make the reasons for Grieve's worry his business also.

She seemed to read his thought and gave him a slow smile. "I suppose McLean told you that your father always ate with Dad and me."

He shook his head, thinking that perhaps there were a great many matters McLean had not told him about.

"For a while I want to eat with the rest to see how the food is in the men's mess," Keegan said.

Laraine laughed. "That's exactly what it is!"

He watched her walk away, observing the easy swing of her body longer than he had intended. Two teamsters going toward the commissary saw him and grinned at each other.

"The Sunshine Kid is in for trouble," one laughed.

For a while the name puzzled Keegan, and then he remembered Albo's tanned chest and arms.

—CHAPTER NINE—

The chill of a clear night was settling over the desert when McLean and Derwent came to Keegan's tent, a small one not far removed from the quarters of Grieve and his daughter.

Liash Keegan had not pampered himself; the tent held a bale of hay for a seat, a cot with two brown blankets for covers and a folded coat for a pillow. While shaking the dust off the coat, Keegan had dislodged two letters written by his mother to his father.

He had put them back with a packet of others in an inside pocket of the coat; and with them he had put the letter that had started him toward this desolate country beyond the end of track.

That was the extent of all the paper work he intended to do on the entire job.

Under a smoking lantern suspended from the ridge pole of the tent, Derwent and McLean sat on the hay and waited for Keegan to speak.

"First thing tomorrow I'm going to get

some dynamite from Capps," Keegan said.

"That'll be a good trick if you can do it."
Derwent's tight mouth twisted. He hadn't
bothered to get his ear sewed up, Keegan
noticed. "If you ask me, Capps is the boy
who's trying to ruin this layout!"

"Don't let your suspicions get away just
because you hate his guts," McLean said.
"Because he fired you —"

Derwent swung his head belligerently.
"Who do *you* think it is?"

"When I get to thinking that close I
won't be talking about it." McLean eyed
Derwent with the same cold detachment
he had given Mike during what might have
been Mike's last few moments on earth.

Keegan watched the two men closely. It
was Derwent who looked away first.

"Here's what I want," Keegan said.
"Derwent, I want you to run the job and
keep the men going. McLean will take care
of the business end just the same as before.
I'll be somewhere in the middle, doing
what I can. I'll back up anything either of
you do — outside of pick handle stuff.

"Both of you have got experience that I
lack. I'm telling you now I'm going to run
this thing and be the boss, but I'm depending
on you two to keep me straight if I get any
wild ideas. That's about the size of it."

"All right," Derwent said. "The first thing I'm going to do is get on Grieve."

"I'll handle him myself," Keegan said.

Derwent stared, and then his mouth twisted in an evil grin and his eyes showed thoughts that made Keegan want to grab him by the throat.

Keegan held his anger. "I bluffed the cook today and got away with it, and I was lucky. But I'm not taking a chance on getting rough with Grieve and losing a blacksmith when we can worst afford it."

McLean nodded. "There ain't no better blacksmith — when he's himself."

Derwent glared as if to ask what a combination storekeeper and timekeeper would know about such matters.

"Beginning tonight I want the guards on the water tank and at the horse yard changed at midnight. A full night is too much for anyone to go without falling asleep." Keegan looked at Derwent.

The superintendent nodded. "That's what happened the night someone cut the hose. I'll see it's done."

"Tomorrow I want to go over the job with you, Derwent — after I come back with the dynamite." Keegan hoped his face didn't show that he hadn't the least idea how he was going to deal with Capps.

Derwent looked at McLean. "By God! I believe he means it about the powder, Mac!"

"I sure do," Keegan said, watching McLean's eyes.

An hour later, having prowled the camp restlessly, checking the guards, looking for possible fire hazards, Keegan returned to his quarters ready for bed.

He saw someone standing just outside Grieve's tent, yellow light from the open flaps lying dimly on his back. After a moment Keegan decided it was the blacksmith himself.

"Got a bellows-boy picked out?" he asked.

Grieve didn't seem to hear. He was staring into the night, toward where a white horse was a bulky shadow in the gloom. Keegan heard the sound of Laraine's voice and then a man's low-voiced laugh.

That would be Albo out there with her, Keegan thought.

"I'll get someone — until I catch up with the work." Grieve turned slowly and walked into his tent.

Keegan stayed a few moments longer, looking toward the horse. None of my business, he tried to tell himself, but the thought wouldn't stick.

The yells of drunken revelers came faintly from the direction of Albo's camp.

Keegan was scowling as he got ready for bed.

Before sunrise he was on Bear Trap, headed for Capps' camp, armed with no more than a vague plan that had a lot of weak spots in it. He neared McLean washing on a bench near the water tank.

"Off to the wars on an empty belly?" McLean asked. He began to dry his face on a clean towel.

"I'll eat breakfast with Brother Capps."

"Be ready to pay for it if he sees you." McLean wrapped the towel around his neck. "Want some help?"

Keegan shook his head and rode on.

Albo's tents showed no life. He stared thoughtfully at a white horse picketed near one of the smaller tents.

The group Keegan joined near one of Capps' mess tents was bunched, jammed, and ready to strike hard when the time came. A sad-eyed bull-cook untied the tent flaps and leaped for his life. Keegan went in with the surge; he couldn't have done otherwise.

Tin plates were nailed to the planks, even closer than the ones had been in

Keegan's camp. Eating was a matter of wrist action and head ducking, so closely packed was the mess.

"How come the nailed plates?" Keegan asked the man on his right.

"Get more men at a table that way," the fellow answered through a mouthful of food.

Breakfast consisted of thick slabs of side meat that looked and tasted old; pieces of bread torn by hand from loaves tossed on the table by hangdog bull-cooks; thick pancakes not always cooked clear through, with syrup thinner than the skimmed howl of a lonesome cat; and cups of bitter coffee.

Keegan ignored the greasy film left on his plate from previous meals and ate well. With difficulty he extricated himself from between his two immediate companions.

He was looking the camp over when he heard Capps' rumbling voice behind him. "Did you bring my water and the two flies?" Capps' tiny eyes were glinting with humor.

Keegan grinned. "Next trip." He watched Capps load stuff. Rough as the man was, Keegan sided with McLean in the belief that Capps was not the kind to resort to sneaky tricks to get something he wanted.

"And now you owe me for a hearty breakfast — Mister Keegan." Capps emphasized the name heavily.

"The word gets around fast," Keegan said, grinning.

"I sort of figured yesterday you wasn't no average boomer — even if you don't look one bit like Liash."

"Kind words won't change my mind about needing dynamite, part of what you highgraded. I need it, Capps."

Capps spat deliberately between his big, wide-spread feet. "Ever try plowing that rock, Keegan?"

"This ain't Nebraska, Capps."

Capps cocked his head a little as he scratched through sandy hair that was crowding one ear. "I found that out."

They measured each other quietly.

The faint trace of a smile showed on Capps' wide face. "I ain't got no ton of powder in my hip pocket," he said, working a few grains of snuff off his under lip.

"So that's how much you swiped from me?"

"Two, three boxes less than a ton," Capps said. "I'll send it over in a few days, no longer than a week."

"I can't wait that long," Keegan said.

Capps' upper lip twitched. "Help yourself to any you can find on this job — if you feel like it."

Keegan considered the challenge. It was exactly what he had expected. He looked at a group of five big, hard-eyed men, obviously foremen, who were waiting to speak to Capps. Common sense told Keegan that he wouldn't get far if he asked for a showdown.

"All right, Capps. Pay me back in a few days."

For a moment Capps appeared to be disappointed at the retreat. Then he nodded curtly and turned to the waiting men.

Keegan walked up the street between tents, stopping when he saw a man come from a large tent, clenching his hands in new leather gloves. Glancing back over his shoulder, Keegan saw that Capps was walking away.

Men were hurrying to make last-minute purchases at the commissary before going to work. Where the rough counter turned in an L that nearly blocked one end of the tent, Keegan saw a tall, bald, black-bearded man sitting at a packing case desk littered with papers. He walked down the room and leaned across the counter.

"When in tarnation are we going to get

that dynamite?" he asked.

The bald man didn't look up. "Should be here this morning," he said.

"Is Pete hauling it?" Keegan asked.

The bald man looked up, scratching at his beard with a pencil. "Pete? — Who's Pete? Turkey Wilson is bringing it in." He gave Keegan close scrutiny. "You're a new foreman around here, ain't you? You'd better not let Capps catch you asking questions when you ought to be out with your men."

Keegan nodded and walked away quickly.

—CHAPTER TEN—

Sitting on Bear Trap at the top of Coyote Hill, Keegan saw a high wheeler moving slowly toward him across the lava flats. He waited until the driver pulled the hill and stopped to breathe his horses.

Except that he lacked a mustache, the teamster who greeted Keegan might have been the same man he had helped up the hill the day before. He was weather-beaten, long-necked, and his Adam's apple ran the same circuit.

"Hello, Wilson," Keegan said.

The teamster spat from the corner of his mouth, squinting at Keegan. "I ain't saw you before. You got me mixed up with my brother?"

"Maybe I have," Keegan said. "You favor him."

"I'm Turkey."

"I'm Keegan."

"Liash's boy?"

Keegan nodded.

"Well, now! I'm right glad to know you. Me 'n' Liash have kicked around together more 'n' once." Turkey stopped in the middle of a wide grin to squint appraisingly. "You ain't so hefty as him, are you?"

Keegan grinned. "I'm beginning to think not."

Turkey was full of questions about Liash and full of talk about a good many other subjects, so it was some time before Keegan could get around to his problem. He explained what Capps had done.

"Suppose you rode this mule in real slow while I was driving off with that load of dynamite?"

Turkey considered. He grinned and spat. "You're talking sense, Keegan! If old Capps wants to get sore and beller, guess me and my brother can drive for most any old contractor we pick. Get up here and take these lines!"

Keegan climbed the wheel and Turkey leaped down.

"Go right past the camp," Turkey said. "Capps hangs around the shop twice a day — in the middle of the morning and the middle of the afternoon — but for a while he'll be walking the job."

Bear Trap tried two bites before Turkey got mounted. Turkey laughed. "Nice hunk of baling wire, this mule!" As Keegan started the team downhill Turkey yelled,

"Don't throw any matches in that bucket of oats under the seat! There's a thousand caps in it!"

Sensing a new hand on the lines, the horses took Keegan and his cargo bouncing down the rocky hill a great deal faster than he cared to go, but once on the level he got the team under control.

Turkey rode alongside and laughed. "Some folks think dynamite goes off at the drop of a hat. Why, I've turned my rig over with loads of it!"

Turkey began to drop behind as they neared Capps' camp. A teamster examining a lame horse watched Keegan curiously as he drove by the herd yard. "Hey!" he yelled. "Ain't that Turk Wilson's rig?"

"Just bought it from him," Keegan said. He drove on. The teamster watched for a while, then turned his attention back to the lame animal.

Close to his own camp, Keegan saw Derwent moving among men loading dump wagons in a cut. He stood up and faced the superintendent, who stared until he recognized Keegan. Then Derwent brought two men and came on the run.

McLean came out of his quarters when the freighter pulled into camp. He showed no surprise when Keegan told him what he had. "Better store it in the commissary," McLean said. "If we leave it out that'll mean one more man to guard it."

In a short time the five men had the dynamite stowed in one end of the commissary tent, just outside the hay partition that formed one wall of McLean's quarters.

"A heck of a place for dynamite," one of the men said. McLean showed no concern over having a ton of explosives stored less than fifteen feet from his cot. "The stuff will be all right," he said.

Standing outside with Derwent and the two men he had brought with him, Keegan looked toward the blacksmith's shop and listened to gratifying sounds of industry therein. "How's the steel this morning, Derwent?"

"Good," the superintendent said, and then in the same voice, "Get set, Keegan."

Capps was riding into camp astride a bulky brown workhorse that appeared strong enough to pull over a full-grown oak.

"Watch him," Derwent said. "He'll stand flatfooted with a half-grin on his face and knock you pizzle-end-up the next second."

"Go on back to work," Keegan said.

Capps turned his head slowly to watch Derwent and the two drillers as they went by him. Derwent hesitated a moment, surveying the burly construction boss with a savage stare that Capps returned without expression.

He rode up to Keegan and dismounted heavily. He stood watching the younger man a few moments, then moved one thumb in a slow gesture toward the drillers and Derwent. "You don't care how tough they come, do you?"

"I need tough men," Keegan said.

Capps smiled faintly, glancing toward Turkey Wilson's team and wagon. "Got any powder to spare?"

"Ever try plowing that rock, Capps?"

Capps rubbed the shaggy fringe of hair above one ear and almost smiled openly, but his tiny eyes were hard and steady. "I could come take that powder."

"It might not be worth it," Keegan said.

Capps considered. "Maybe." He spat between his feet. "I didn't figure on it — this time."

They eyed each other carefully, Keegan remembering Derwent's warning about Capps being dangerous when he was quiet and smiling. From the corner of his eye Keegan saw McLean standing in the entrance to the commissary.

From the blacksmith's shop came the sounds of pumping bellows, hammer blows, and a mournful voice singing a doleful song about a lad who had gone down the primrose path but who was welcome home anyway, if anybody happened to know where he was roistering at the moment and would be kind enough to tell him.

"Your gag worked," Capps said. "Once is enough."

"We're even," Keegan said.

"We'll call it that for the time." Head thrust forward slightly, Capps moved his lower lip gently around his load of snuff. He turned slowly, mounted the saddleless brown horse and rode out of camp.

McLean took his right hand out of his pocket and said calmly, "The only thing he respects is the same kind of treatment he dishes out to others. If he'd been minded to take the dynamite, he'd've said so — and then come after it."

Maybe, Keegan thought, wondering if McLean and Derwent weren't trying to characterize Capps as a good deal less subtle than the man really was.

He walked over to the blacksmith's shop.

Grieve had a helper; a small, sharp-eyed man pumping the bellows. He broke off his song about the erring lad just as the parents had given up general pleas to humanity and had turned the case over to higher authorities.

The blacksmith looked at Keegan over a red-hot drill bit and nodded. He fashioned the bit deftly, gauging it to extra width for soft, fitchery rock; he threw it on a pile with others lying on the floor and pulled another drill from the forge.

The bit was sparkling hot. Grieve turned angrily on his helper. "Burn another one like that and I'll wrap it around your head."

The smith squinted at the bit he held, decided it wasn't too hot to take a chance on. He began to sharpen it. "The coal is bad," he said. "But we'll get by."

Unless Grieve had been deliberately sloughing off, the blacksmith's shop would be all right, Keegan thought. He stepped outside, looking beyond the water tank to where Capps had halted and was talking to Turkey Wilson on Bear Trap. The teamster laughed in a squealing voice and came riding on toward camp.

"See if you can get that skinner to haul for us," McLean called. "Freighters have been a wee bit leery of their money since your Dad left."

Turkey Wilson rode up laughing. "Capps said I'd probably have to buy my team and rig back from you." He frowned. "He told me to tell you you had a darn good black-smith. What was he getting at there?"

Keegan shook his head. He had come to the conclusion that whatever Capps said had a very definite meaning that wasn't always easy to grasp.

He grinned at Turkey. "How about freighting for us? Hard work, no whisky — and get your money three years after the rails are down."

Turkey squealed his laugh. "Just the way I like it, except the no-whisky part. I'll get my brother too."

McLean almost smiled. "Come in here, Turkey," he said.

For a while Keegan stood where he was, looking around the camp. He saw that the hay had been properly stacked and protected by canvas; the clutter of tools around the blacksmith's shop was diminishing; at the rear of the mess tent the two bull cooks were throwing tin cans and other trash into a dump cart, and the fat cook himself was supervising in a clean apron.

Keegan knew without looking that no drunks were lying in the bunk tents today. He'd had a lot of luck in establishing his authority. His hell-raising yesterday and his outwitting of Capps today were the sort of actions that would gain him the respect of the men, a condition that would last only as long as he was man enough to make it last.

The job was still here to beat — and with it the man or men who had outwitted Liash Keegan and everybody else.

His next move would be to go over the work, find out how much money he could expect to make from yardage moved, and how long it would take to finish the contract. But before doing anything he decided to take off his heavy coat, which was becoming unbearably hot.

He went to his tent and left the garment. When he emerged Laraine Grieve was coming out of her tent with a bundle of clothes. She smiled at him. "I see you've taken hold of things."

Keegan grinned. "I've won a couple of small pots."

She walked with him on her way to the water tank, going on alone when he stopped to mount Bear Trap.

"They'll probably come a little tougher from now on," she called back.

He caught up with her and rode alongside. "What do you mean?" he asked.

Her smile told him nothing except that she had good teeth. "I mean you haven't run into any trouble yet," she said.

Keegan wasn't sure just what she did mean.

—CHAPTER ELEVEN—

Derwent was supervising removal of rock in the same cut where black powder had heaved up the huge chunk. Scrapermen were bucking what loose rock there was, cursing and sweating as the scoops jolted and twisted and finally gathered in a few broken fragments. Every scraper that made a trip without moving a full load was losing money — and no scoop was getting even one third of a load.

"It's this or work it by hand," Derwent said. "And either way you still got the horses to feed."

Keegan nodded, looking at drillers slanting in dry, shallow holes. Water, he thought, wouldn't stay long in this keyed-together, semi-loose formation. The holes already down, more than a score of them, were marked with rock chips laid across the collars to prevent loose material from being kicked into the holes.

They were well placed for maximum breaking.

"The dynamite will help," Derwent said.

"But even at that half the shots pot-hole or blow down into a loose seam." He mopped his brown forehead. "If you know where to borrow, you'd better be figuring on it, because old Paul Bunyan himself couldn't rip enough yardage out of this to meet the next payroll."

Keegan studied the superintendent carefully, wondering if Derwent was making a bid to find out whether or not the company had enough money to meet the next payroll. According to McLean, only he and Liash Keegan had known how much gold arrived in camp the night Liash was wounded.

Stroud might have guessed — or perhaps Liash had told him. McLean wasn't sure about that. Firing Stroud, Keegan thought, had been a mistake, unavoidable perhaps, but still a mistake that he would have avoided if he could have.

"I'll borrow if I have to — if I can," Keegan said.

"I'll do my best to make it here," Derwent said. "But when an outfit don't pay off in this country" — he shook his head and grinned his twisted grin — "it just ain't a sad case of polite bankruptcy; it's murder!"

Derwent gestured toward the sweating,

cursing men. Several of them were wearing guns; a huge, shaggy-haired hammerman, his face gray from drill dust, was standing on one leg while cutting free a loose boot sole by means of a six-inch knife blade that glinted in the sun.

"When it comes time to pay, they want their money," Derwent said.

"I don't blame them." Keegan dismounted and dropped the reins. "Let's walk along and look things over."

Keegan made no show of his own incomplete but sound knowledge of yardage and engineers' estimates. He listened carefully to Derwent and learned a great deal more, somewhat amazed at Derwent's capacity for quick mental figuring. They examined a mile of the work and at the end Keegan had to admit to himself that he could see no way of meeting the next payroll from estimates of moved yardage.

Keegan pointed at the camel-backed hill near Albo's camp. "I suppose that's solid rock and smack on the line?"

Derwent grinned. "I haven't looked it over yet, but you can bet the engineers didn't run in no curve just to miss a hill."

Keegan went on alone to look at the hill and Derwent went toward the west end of the job. Walking through the heat, Keegan thought that Derwent was an excellent prospect as the troublemaker. The man was smart, knew construction, and could take an outfit and make money — if the contracts farther west were what they were cracked up to be.

An hour later, having forced Bear Trap a little faster than the mule cared to travel, Keegan was watching McLean looking for a copy of contract specifications. McLean found what he wanted and studied it, then handed the papers to Keegan.

Keegan grinned. "Rock, she says. Every inch of it is to be paid for at rock prices."

He explained to McLean that the hill was far from solid. The edges of it were rock and there were some solid ribs in it, but most of it was formed of loose material that had drifted against the camel-back and settled down through years of weather into a solid-appearing mass.

The engineers' bull in classification was common and not serious — but it might prove enough to save Liash Keegan's outfit after the money now hidden in McLean's quarters had been largely expended on the next payday.

"We'll hold it as an ace in the hole," Keegan said.

He was still thinking of that hill just

before he went to sleep that night.

Wild cowboy shouts waked him in the middle of the night. He grabbed his gun from under his father's coat and kicked the blankets off.

He was feeling for his boots when the tent came down around him. Someone whooped. The sound of hooves grew loud. Keegan threshed under the canvas, his sense of direction lost entirely. And then he heard the beating of hundreds of iron-shod hooves and he knew that someone was driving the herd. He pushed canvas away with both hands and tried to walk from under it. The next moment he was sprawled across a bale of hay and had lost his gun.

On his knees, he gathered canvas toward him with both hands, throwing it over his back. Then he felt cold air strong against his face and saw dim light from the starry sky.

He saw a shadowy rider, heard him whoop. On both sides of the fallen tent animals were streaming past. Straight ahead was a solid black mass, the bulk of the herd. They were coming hard at the fallen tent. He had glimpses of riders on the outside of the herd.

Those animals were bunched closely and

held that way by the night riders. In a few moments his tent was going to be trampled.

Rocks bruised his bare feet as he ran. From somewhere near Grieve's tent a rifle spoke in two quick flat blasts. Forerunners of the stampeding herd were still breaking around the fallen shelter, instinctively shying away from the canvas.

Running shoulder to shoulder, a mule and a horse jostled each other. The horse stumbled and fell. Keegan moved in long leaps. He was astride the horse when it regained its feet.

And then the surge and thunder of fear-maddened animals was all around him, slamming against him hard.

Hairy bodies raked against his legs. His mount, not yet in stride, was jostled and staggered and almost fell. Keegan twisted his fingers in its mane and stayed aboard. From both flanks of the herd came more wild, quavering yells. He caught sight of a flapping blanket.

He lay low against the neck of his mount and rode.

Streaks of flame ripped the darkness as the night raiders fired. Keegan raised his head. They were firing in the air, he decided. And then he saw a blossoming explosion that momentarily lit up the arm of a man holding his gun high.

The riders swept away into the night. Quavering Rebel yells marked their going, grew fainter. The herd began to scatter and slow down. Keegan found himself several hundred yards out into the night, astride a trembling horse that slowed to a limping trot and then finally stopped of its own accord.

Hundreds of voices were raised in a wild uproar from the camp. After Keegan slapped his horse around and neared the tents he could distinguish Derwent's bellow above the rest. The superintendent was yelling for men to catch stray horses and round up the herd.

Someone shot at Keegan as he loomed up from the outer darkness. He shouted angrily and heard McLean cursing someone. Lanterns began to move jerkily around the tents.

Ignoring the bedlam of questions from excited men, Keegan rode to his own tent. A bearded teamster in red woolens was holding a lantern high, looking at a long lumpish shape under ripped canvas.

"They squashed the boss right in his own bed!" he said in a tone more of awe than regret.

"That's hay!" Keegan said. He began to look for his clothes. When McLean appeared with a lantern a moment later Keegan asked, "Where was the night guard?"

"He'd just gone to one of the bunk tents to wake his relief," McLean said.

Someone handed Keegan one of his boots. He found his pants and began to put them on. Men were untangling the wreckage to find his other possessions. "This rifle stock's busted," someone commented.

The raid had been timed to the second, Keegan thought. Until two nights before the herd guard had been on duty a full shift, but the riders had known that arrangements had been changed.

He saw Grieve with a rifle. A moment later Laraine came to stand by her father. She was fully dressed.

"Was that you who shot?" Keegan asked Grieve, who nodded without enthusiasm.

"Did you hit anybody or get a good look at anyone?" McLean asked.

Grieve shook his head curtly. "All I did was manage to kill one of our own horses," he said gloomily.

Keegan saw Laraine look away and smile. He himself was in no smiling mood.

At dawn Derwent reported that all but fifteen head had been rounded up. "Just a few of the spooky ones went very far," he said. "We'll have to find 'em before Capps does, or he'll grab 'em and put 'em to work and give us one devil of an argument before we get 'em back."

The superintendent scratched at one meaty jowl. "The way I dope those tracks, a blamed handy bunch of riders done this job."

"They weren't dirt-stiffs riding work plugs," Keegan said. He remembered that the last time he'd heard Rebel yells had been on the Staked Plains.

Derwent went back to check on the herd and Keegan walked out on the plain, trying to find the place where he had seen the unusual burst of flame from a gun. He walked in an expanding circle and was about to give up when he caught a bright flash showing fifty yards away.

He walked over and picked up a cheap suicide special, powder-blackened around the hammer where the frame had cracked from the revolver's last shot. No wonder, he thought, there had been a gush of fire and the man had dropped the weapon. He probably had a painfully burned hand at least.

Keegan examined the gun closely. It was stamped by dies to simulate engraving. Two pieces of buckhorn had been crudely fitted to replace the original butt grips and give a much larger grasping surface for the hand.

What interested him most was the stamped name on the metal: *Prairie Giant.*

According to the old trackworker at Yankee Falls, Walker had been killed by either a Prairie Giant or a Little Demon. If this was the gun, Keegan thought, it should have blown up when aimed at Walker.

The buckhorn grips, incongruously large for so small a gun, came two inches below his hand when he held the weapon.

He heard Laraine calling his name and saw her standing before her tent. "How about some coffee?" she called.

Keegan dropped the revolver into his pocket and walked toward the girl.

—CHAPTER TWELVE—

For two weeks Keegan told no one about the Prairie Giant.

Brawny hammermen beat steel under the hot sun. Dynamite ripped and tore at lava rock, sometimes breaking along irregular cleavage lines with negligible results; rattlesnakes crawled angrily from shattered retreats to add more hazard to the work; Derwent and his foremen, who had caught some of his driving spirit, pushed scrapermen and clean-up crews to moving fragments almost before the last pieces from the blasts had fallen.

True to his word, Derwent was fighting hard to make yardage that would meet the payroll. The swaggering superintendent crowded the crews hard; he pushed and bullied, fighting those who wanted to fight, bluffing those who were afraid. He threatened and he cursed; he wore a gun and forgot about pick handles, but one day when two husky shovelmen jumped him he beat them both in rough and tumble fighting without touching his weapon.

He was getting the work done.

On the adjoining contract east, fourteen miles of it, Capps' crews were working even harder. Bitterly won fill began to grow. Engineers came by on both jobs and probed the grade with bullpricks to determine if outsize rocks had been thinly covered in the backfill. They set finish grade stakes where fill was high or low, and if the variation was not too great both Capps and Keegan drove down or raised the stakes to match the grade already built.

"You'd think a tenth of an inch meant life or death to those Buckrams," Derwent snarled.

Flatcar loads of ties and steel pushed west. Gandys dug and maulmen swung. The sounds of steel on steel went a little closer every day toward an ocean somewhere hundreds of miles away. Romanticists talked in glowing terms of shining rails binding a continent. Promoters talked of freight to haul, of money to make, and cut each other's throats in financial manipulations.

Contractors talked of estimates that wouldn't meet their expenses, and wondered how free Western banks were with their money.

Those who built the railroad talked of women and whisky, mixing sweat and curses with each shovelful or scraper load of lava rock.

Contractors between Capps and Yankee Falls finished their work and moved west or went broke and lost their outfits. For every four that went west to promised land, three lost everything, including their lives sometimes, when enraged workers took revenge for money owed.

One small operator, his wife and two small sons were killed one night when unpaid, drunken men burned and looted the camp.

Penalties for delaying track crews fell heavily on some. The Oregon Short Line was costing far more than would ever be paid for it.

But the rails fell farther west.

And with their coming came also a free haulage of supplies and water for contractors still holding out. Freighting costs went down for Keegan as the end of track came closer. Turkey Wilson and his brother, Long Neck, worked night and day bringing water, food, and the always rapidly consumed feed for horses and mules.

Mike Uri and his partner, Sam Johns — the two men Keegan had sent to the hills for deer meat — began to deliver venison every four days. They sold the haunches to

Keegan for three cents a pound and the rest of the meat went into Capps' cooking pots at one cent a pound.

From a Capps scraperman who had been fired for using a full, fresh pan of water to wash his face and hands, Keegan learned that Capps had hired Stroud as a foreman, and that Stroud had lasted one week, having been fired for starting a fight one night in a bunk tent — a fight that expanded into a free-for-all during which a broken lantern set the tent afire.

"Stroud wasn't like that — bad to fight," McLean commented, his implication clear as he looked at Keegan.

"Until I came, you mean?"

"He was touchy about the job then — that's what caused you and him trouble, but now he's sore at the world." McLean paused. "Your father thought a lot of Stroud."

"I've got a super now," Keegan said curtly, trying to conceal his own feelings about the firing of Stroud. Just because the man looked a little like a long-dead son of Liash Keegan. . . . Still, Liash must have been lonely for the boy who had died and the one he had disowned.

"It was Stroud's own fault," Keegan said, and he knew by McLean's keen look that the storekeeper was seeing beyond words again. But McLean let the subject lie.

"Did you ever see anyone around Albo's with a burned hand like the one you had me check for here in camp?" McLean asked.

Keegan shook his head. He hadn't told McLean about the broken Prairie Giant when he had ordered the storekeeper to check unobtrusively to see if anyone in camp had a powder-seared hand. Keegan was sure that the night raiders who had scattered the herd were outsiders, but still he had wanted to be sure, because in the excitement some of his own men could have done the job, mingling with others rounding up the broken herd a few minutes later.

Keegan himself had spent several evenings watching men at Albo's, but he hadn't seen anyone with a burned hand.

He had seen plenty of fights, and he had talked twice to Albo, each time noticing that the handsome, pale-faced man was showing dislike for Keegan, a fact not hard to understand when one considered that Laraine was visiting less and less with Albo on the edge of Keegan's camp, and talking to Keegan more and more at every opportunity.

"Did Stroud know how much money you brought into camp?" Keegan had asked McLean.

The storekeeper's eyes showed nothing. "He could have guessed it. He didn't know what Liash got from the bank, but he'd helped Liash bring in gold before and could judge the weight, I suppose." McLean shrugged. "As I said before, maybe Liash told him."

Keegan nodded, wondering if McLean's concern over Stroud's discharge went any deeper than personal liking for the man. Anyway, Keegan thought, after another week and payday there wouldn't be enough gold left in McLean's quarters to cause any great worry.

Lying on his cot that night, Keegan considered his chances of beating the job and his enemies. To do the first would automatically include the second, but he wouldn't be satisfied until he had both tasks sewed up in a bag. He had begun to accept McLean's belief that the shooting of Liash Keegan might be in no way connected with the trouble in camp.

Four or five men had stampeded the herd. That a gang was trying to break the company and get control of it was not a sound theory, Keegan thought, because a group of reckless, hard-riding men probably would be more tempted to rob contractors of payrolls.

But someone could have hired the four or five riders, someone who had money to pay them and money to buy and handle the Keegan Construction Company if it went bust. Only Albo and Capps seemed to fit. The saloonman was making money hand over fist; Capps was a big contractor, supposed to have made a fortune on Nebraska jobs.

And still neither one of them entirely satisfied Keegan as a suspect. Why should Albo, who had a sure thing, take on the uncertain joy and certain grief of running a construction company? All he had to do was follow up the jobs with his whisky and gambling, making money the easy way.

Capps was already expanded to the point where his organization was so large it was hard to control. He had ceased to buy up equipment of bankrupt contractors since Keegan arrived.

Derwent had been working for a dollar and a half a day when Keegan gave him the super's job; Grieve was a blacksmith without resources; McLean was getting fifty dollars a month as storekeeper and timekeeper; Stroud had been a foreman getting twenty-five cents more a day than the men — until Liash Keegan had been shot.

The outfit was worth at least forty thousand. But if it had to be sold, the horses, equipment — tools, plows, graders, scrapers, tents and the rest — might not bring one fourth of their value.

Of the men Keegan had considered, only two appeared to be likely to have enough money to take over the company — and those two seemed to have little reason to want the outfit.

Still, the hard fact was there: someone had been trying to hamstring the company since the start of the job. Liash Keegan undoubtedly had enemies, but a man bent on revenge was not likely to take the long way in an effort to get even. No wonder McLean had shaken his head and said he didn't understand; no wonder Liash had been driven to rages.

The next morning Keegan ate breakfast with Laraine and her father. Grieve plainly didn't like the arrangement and showed his displeasure by being curt, watching every glance between Keegan and the girl from deep-set, brooding eyes. Keegan had sensed for some time that the blacksmith considered no man on earth quite good enough for his daughter.

He was planning to send Laraine east to school as soon as he had saved enough money; she had told Keegan that she didn't want to go. With the normal vanity of man he attributed her decision at least in small part to his own presence.

"What did Albo do before he started running a saloon?" Keegan asked. Laraine gave him a quick look.

Grieve scowled at his coffee. "He was a railroad contractor. Went busted in Texas on a big job."

Keegan saw Laraine watching him closely. "So he turned to easy money after that?"

"Dirty money!" Grieve said.

Keegan saw that the girl's color had heighted a little. "Maybe he doesn't like to beat his head against lava rock for nothing," she said.

"You lose or win honest that way," Grieve said. He started to say more, but glanced at Keegan and was silent.

Suspicion about Albo lay heavily in Keegan's mind as he finished the meal in silence.

Laraine followed him outside. They were silent while Grieve walked slowly toward the blacksmith's tent.

"I'm going in today," Laraine said. "Anything you want from town?"

Keegan barely heard the question. "Does Albo intend to follow these jobs right on west — like a parasite?"

She gave him a cool, level look. "I don't know, but if you're afraid to speak right out with what you're thinking, I'll tell you this: Several times I've urged Carson to quit the saloon business and go back to contracting — and maybe he will."

Keegan mulled that over in silence.

"Do you want anything from town?"

Keegan eyed the girl steadily. "Yes — one favor."

He went to his tent and came back with the Prairie Giant. Laraine looked at it curiously. "That's a cheap-looking piece of junk."

"It didn't show its cheapness soon enough," Keegan said bitterly. "If you don't mind, I'd like you to take this down to the station in Yankee Falls. You'll find an old duck puttering around there with a spike maul — if he isn't around the agent —"

"I'll find him," she said.

"I don't know exactly how to do it best — but I'd like to find out if the old boy ever saw this gun before. If he has, he probably won't talk about it, but his face will tell."

She smiled and her dark eyes lit with humor lights. "He might talk to me — if you haven't already scared him to death." She took the gun and, still smiling, walked into her tent.

Keegan watched the sway of her body until she was out of sight and then glanced toward Albo's tents with a frown.

It came to him that he might be making a foolish mistake.

Derwent came striding toward him from the blacksmith's shop. "I found the last two horses all right. They was in Capps' herd and he'd been working the tar out of 'em." Derwent cursed the burly contractor. "I almost near had a fight with him before we got 'em back."

It struck Keegan that Derwent, snarly as he was, might not hate Capps as violently as he pretended.

—CHAPTER THIRTEEN—

At dusk when sounds of loud revelry were just beginning to drift from Albo's tents, Keegan saw Mike Uri and Johns pull into camp with a load of deer meat and stop behind the cook shack.

His senses receptive to sounds of anything that concerned stores or company money, McLean was on the spot immediately. Derwent came out of one of the bunk tents and walked toward the wagon. By the time Keegan arrived the cook was weighing saddles on a stillyard balance and McLean was recording weights.

Keegan drew Uri aside, after both Mike and Johns had stared at Derwent with looks of bitter, burning hatred.

"How many deer camps back in the hills?" Keegan asked.

"Plenty of 'em," Mike said.

"All meat hunters?" From the corner of his eye Keegan saw Grieve arrive.

Mike's attention, partly distracted in challenging stares at Derwent, now came fully on Keegan. "There's a few camps of floaters — the payroll crowd, the hunters call 'em."

"Anybody you know?" Keegan asked.

Mike's eyes narrowed. He cast a calculating glance on Derwent. "Yeah — Boxcar Branson. He's there."

Keegan saw that everybody was listening now. "Who's he?"

"He's the fellow that Liash fired for busting a new plow," McLean said. He didn't take his eyes from the balance. "Fifteen pounds even on that one," he said to Johns.

"Boxcar ain't hunting for the camps," Mike said. He kept looking at Derwent. "But I helped him skin a deer one day because he had a bad hand."

Keegan felt his stomach muscles tighten. "Sprain?"

"Burned when he was reloading shells, he said."

"It's a wonder he didn't get that big nose and jaw burnt," Grieve said. "They was always sticking out into somebody's business — like the time he busted the plow and tried to tell me the point wasn't tempered right."

Keegan's mind leaped instantly to the brown-faced man he had seen playing poker at Albo's. "What's this Boxcar look like?" he asked Mike.

Uri jerked his thumb at Derwent. "Ask him. They was partners."

McLean called another weight. Keegan watched the hard glare of hatred Derwent gave Mike.

"Boxcar and me fell in together on the way down here from Montana," Derwent said. "Old Liash hired us the same day after we had trouble with Capps." He looked at Keegan. "Boxcar's kind of a sawed-off runt with a big brown face and a nose and jaw like Grieve said. Last time I see him at Albo's he said he was hunting for the track layers."

"He ain't now," Mike said. "He's with the payroll crowd."

Keegan tried to conceal his thoughts. The facts fitted together pretty well, he decided. Boxcar was riding with a wild bunch, the sort of men who could be hired for a little hell-raising like scattering a herd. He had a burned hand. He could be the man who had killed Walker.

Keegan remembered that Boxcar had been yawning that afternoon he'd first seen him at Albo's playing poker. Maybe the yawns, like the bartender's, had been from heat — and maybe from the fact that he had ridden all night from Yankee Falls.

Whether or not Derwent fitted into the trouble with Boxcar was another matter that would be hard to determine; but the fact was large and hard: if Boxcar had killed Walker, the brown-faced man certainly knew who was the inside man behind trouble in Keegan's camp.

Just by a breath he kept from asking about the type of gun Boxcar had had.

The man who came into camp a moment later was spitting blood from where front teeth had been; he was so drunk Keegan wondered how he stayed right side up.

"The gates of hell are open down at Albo's!" he yelled. "We got three foremen laid out cold — crippled! It was the goldarnedest fight —"

"With Capps' crowd?" Derwent demanded.

"Naw!" The messenger weaved on his feet. "We was fighting amongst ourselves for fun." He put his forefinger in the gap where three teeth had been. "But it got a little rough." He named three men, all foremen. "They're crippled."

Derwent cursed. "We'd better take a wagon."

The messenger had been accurate. At the gambling tents Derwent, Grieve and

Keegan loaded three badly used foremen into the wagon. One had a broken leg; one had lost an eye and was still too drunk to know it; the third was still unconscious, so covered with contusions that his specific injuries could not be determined offhand.

From disinterested bystanders Keegan confirmed the courier's statement that the fighting had been largely restricted to his own men beating his own men. He told Derwent to haul the battered cargo back to camp for the cook to work on.

Keegan went looking for Albo.

He found the saloonman watching the wheel-of-fortune in a tent devoted entirely to gambling. The crowd was dense and the money was free, and Keegan thought Albo's line of business certainly had it over contracting — if a man cared for that sort of thing.

Albo was dressed in dark broadcloth, his paleness heightened by the somber garb. His eyes were not friendly when Keegan spoke to him quietly, but he nodded casually and said, "We'll talk in my tent."

With the exception of a canvas wardrobe, Albo's quarters were as rough as Keegan's, a fact which the latter noted with mild surprise. Albo motioned toward a bale of hay. "Make yourself comfortable," he said, smiling as he saw Keegan's reactions to the interior.

Lantern light ran along the part in Albo's coal-black hair as he sat down. The motion revealed to Keegan that the saloonman was wearing a shoulder holster.

"Albo, your whisky is giving me lots of trouble."

"Capps says the same." Albo laughed gently. "So?"

Keegan thought a moment. Albo was on government land and had a government license. He was strictly within his rights. "I suggest you move."

Albo laughed again. "I credit you with better sense than that, Keegan." He studied Keegan carefully. "I know the rest: will I cut down on drinks to those who have too much; will I try to keep men from beating each other up — especially valuable men; and so on.

"I'm not interested in gauging the drinking capacities of men, Keegan. I'm only interested in seeing that they pay for what they get and do their fighting outside."

Keegan controlled his anger. "Your whisky cost me three foremen tonight. I don't want that to happen again."

"Keep your foremen home."

They weighed each other. All the legal

right was on Albo's side; all the moral right was on Keegan's.

"There may be other ways to make you see the light," Keegan said.

Albo's dark eyes were hard and challenging. "Try them all. I did, when an outfit like mine wrecked a job for me in the days when I was in your place. I couldn't lick 'em, so I joined 'em."

"So I heard."

Albo's eyes grew dark as jet. The powerful, driving rivalry of two men over a girl was a solid weight in the looks the two exchanged.

"You work for glory and I'll take mine in money," Albo said.

They let it go at that, but as Keegan walked from the tent he knew he had not finished with Carson Albo.

He started directly toward his own camp. Passing the shadowy bulks of horses tied to a log hitching rack just beyond the edges of light from the tents, Keegan felt the same, cold, dry, spine tingling sensation he had experienced some weeks before at a desolate tank stop.

He peered into the gloom. The dry, raspy voice that whispered his name could belong only to one man.

Whisper Jim came from between two horses. Though Keegan could make out the man's shape and movement, Whisper's words seemed to come out of the night itself. "Liash is getting along. He'll be all right."

The wave of relief that washed through Keegan made him realize how hard he had tried not to worry about his father.

"I was coming by your place a little later, but this'll save me a trip," Whisper said. "I hear you've been having trouble."

"Some," Keegan said.

"If I get some other business I got cleared up in time I'll give you a hand." Whisper glanced toward the horses. "Take good care of Bear Trap. I'll get him later."

He moved away so quietly Keegan couldn't hear the sound of his moccasins.

Instead of striking back to camp at once, Keegan went through the crowded tents, looking for Boxcar Branson. The man was not around.

In the tent Keegan saw Capps and Grieve talking quietly at one end of the crowded bar. The big bald construction boss, his Scotch cap pushed far back on his head, was peering intently at Grieve, who was shaking his head.

Midway in the line that jammed the bar, Keegan saw Stroud. The tall red-head turned as if he had sensed someone was studying him. His face showed healing bruises; his eyes were bloodshot and the hand that held the glass was trembling a little.

He looked squarely at Keegan and showed not the slightest flicker of recognition. Keegan pushed to the bar beside him. "Hello, Stroud."

The big ex-superintendent blinked and ran one hand across puffed lips. "Have a drink," he said thickly.

While Keegan drank his whisky he watched Stroud keenly. The man was not pretending, he decided: he was so far gone he probably didn't know his own name. "Come by the camp and see me tomorrow," Keegan said.

Stroud spilled half his whisky as he tried to drink. "Who're you?"

Keegan looked at a bartender, the same fat-cheeked one who had been dozing the first day Keegan arrived.

"Tell him what I said when he can understand, will you?" Keegan asked.

The bartender looked doubtfully at Stroud, then refilled his glass when the red-head thrust it forward. "It might be a week from now."

"Tell him — whenever it is." Keegan saw Grieve and Capps watching from the end of the bar. Capps was smiling. Grieve met Keegan's gaze a moment and turned his head away quickly.

A few moments later Capps and Grieve went out together. For another half-hour Keegan loitered in first one tent and then another, watching for Boxcar Branson. Three times he met Albo face to face, both men passing without speaking.

Sooner or later Branson would come out of the hills, Keegan thought; and when he did he was due to speak a piece.

Keegan started home.

As he passed the hitching rack he heard two men talking in low tones from near the dark hulk of the animals. One voice was unmistakably the rumbling growl of Penrose Capps.

The other was hoarse and throaty, the voice of Whisper Jim.

Keegan stopped and the voices ceased. He knew two men were looking toward him from the darkness.

He waited a moment and then started the quarter of a mile walk to camp.

—CHAPTER FOURTEEN—

Keegan went directly to McLean's quarters at the back of the commissary. He called the storekeeper's name and started to enter but found the tent flaps tied.

"Just a minute," McLean said. His voice came through the canvas just a few inches away from Keegan, and McLean scarcely had to move to reach the ties.

He had been standing just to one side of the entrance. Keegan watched him cross the room and lay a rifle on the cot. McLean was taking no chances, Keegan thought.

He told the storekeeper what Whisper Jim had said about Liash Keegan, and watched the news bring the first genuine smile he had ever seen on McLean's face.

"What do you make of Whisper?" Keegan asked.

McLean sat down on his cot and shook his head. "I don't know and I don't know anybody that does. From what I gather Whisper is strictly outside the law. He rides alone, and whatever he does he does alone."

"What's his connection with Capps?"

"They're friends — that's all I know. I didn't even know Whisper was Liash's friend until the man popped up from nowhere and took charge of things."

"Any way you can figure Whisper might be our man — the one causing us grief?" Keegan asked.

"After the way he took care of Liash —" McLean's face suddenly went bleak.

For once Keegan knew what McLean was thinking; Keegan was thinking the same thing and didn't like it. "I don't suppose my father was in shape to write himself."

"No," McLean said. "No, he wouldn't be. Of course if we knew for sure —" He shook his head as if the action would kill a thought. "Liash is all right. He's bound to be. We're getting on the wrong track suspecting Whisper, whoever he is. He was on the train going east with Liash when we had our last trouble."

Keegan wanted to believe that too, but he had to admit the possibility that Whisper Jim never had got on the train that took Liash Keegan east.

A happy detachment of drunks coming home early from Albo's raised their shouts on the edge of camp, reminding Keegan of another unsettled problem which he knew no way of handling.

Derwent was extracting the last ounce of work from the outfit; men who went out with hangovers either delivered or were fired, but the strict rule had proved costly. The outfit had lost good men; one teamster apparently all right but with his mind fogged from reveling the night before had wrecked a dump cart; another had crippled a horse; fights were frequent in the camp, the only rule being that contestants do their fighting outside of the tents.

Two men still running bad blood from some trivial incident rising from a drinking bout the night before had started a fight in the mess tent after one jammed his plate of food in the other's face.

Two mess tables had been turned over in the resulting scramble and a hundred men had gone to work without their breakfasts as a result of the food loss.

The job was bad enough without the disrupting influence of Albo's whisky, Keegan thought; but so far he hadn't any idea what to do about the whisky — and so far he hadn't been able to do much about finding the troublemaker in his own camp.

He wondered what luck Laraine was having with the Prairie Giant and the old track worker in Yankee Falls.

"When do you figure on going after the payroll?" McLean asked.

Still involved in his own thoughts, Keegan missed the warning flashed in McLean's eyes. "Since we got the money here already —"

McLean had his rifle and was moving toward the back of the tent. Then Keegan heard footsteps somewhere outside.

Completely nightblind for the instant, the two stood in darkness and listened. They heard no sounds for a few moments, and then boots crunched on lava rock somewhere behind the commissary.

Keegan went around the corner of the tent quickly. More by sound than sight he took long strides toward a dim figure moving toward the open plain. The man stopped. Keegan came close and grasped him by the shoulder.

A powerful hand, warm and work-hardened, fastened on Keegan's arm and a deep voice said, "Easy, mister!"

"Grieve!" Keegan tried to see the blacksmith's face.

"I can't sleep," Grieve said gloomily. "Sometimes I walk for two or three hours."

Whether the smith had been eavesdropping or not was something that asking him was not going to determine, Keegan thought, irritated by his own carelessness.

"Did you notice anyone around the commissary just now?" Keegan asked.

"Somebody was standing near McLean's tent when I went past," Grieve said. Keegan wished he could see the blacksmith's face.

"Who was it?"

"I don't know," Grieve said. "You can find drunks wandering all over this camp at all hours."

"What did Capps want tonight?" Keegan asked bluntly.

Grieve hesitated before answering. "He offered to hire me — it ain't the first time he's done that."

Keegan remembered that Capps had mentioned Grieve's skill as a mechanic to Turkey Wilson the day Capps was riding out of Keegan's camp after the dynamite incident. Maybe, Keegan thought, Capps was as blunt and straightforward as McLean had said; perhaps Capps had been giving advance notice that he was going to try to hire Grieve.

"How are you and Laraine getting along?" Grieve was asking a great deal more than a simple question.

"All right — I guess."

The blacksmith started to say something

150

more, then walked away, the sound of his boots growing fainter as he went straight north on the desolate, snake-infested lava plain.

Back at McLean's tent, Keegan asked, "Did you see or hear anyone?"

McLean shook his head, obviously disgusted at Keegan's slip of the tongue. "I don't go far from this tent at night."

Considering the money stowed in the hay, that wasn't a bad idea, Keegan thought. "This is the first I knew that Grieve couldn't sleep," he said.

"Worry over Laraine and Albo is part of it," McLean said. "But I don't think he ever got over thinking about the money he lost when Liash and him was partners."

Grieve might have been telling the truth about seeing someone near the tent, Keegan reflected. The other man could have walked away quietly, and certainly Grieve had made no pretense of concealing the sound of his own boots.

"Maybe I'd better move into the tent with you," Keegan suggested.

McLean's face showed that he thought himself capable of guarding the gold, but he said, "If you think it's necessary, come ahead."

Keegan considered. Another cot would

crowd the tent badly. McLean was sure of himself and cold-blooded, and he had taken care of almost twice the amount of money by himself. Besides, there was no certainty that anyone knew the gold was there. The man Grieve said he'd seen standing near the tent might have been a drunk wandering aimlessly.

Keegan decided against moving. Unless someone had overheard his careless statement, the only possible person who might know about the gold — other than McLean and himself — would be Stroud.

Perhaps Stroud already had talked too much under the influence of whisky, spilling his thoughts at Albo's for anyone to hear. And again perhaps he hadn't.

Keegan decided not to wait for Stroud to sober up. Instead he would hunt him up in the morning and make an effort to salvage something from his so-far unsatisfactory relationship with the man.

For two hours the next morning Keegan went over the work with Derwent, checking, estimating and figuring. There was no possible way of getting an estimate from the job large enough to meet the payroll.

"You're going to have to borrow," Derwent said.

That made twice, Keegan thought, that

Derwent had mentioned the subject. He wondered again if the superintendent was actually following the popular assumption that the company didn't have a cent left — or whether Derwent was probing for information.

Keegan looked at the camel-backed hill. "Have you thrown a close study on that?" he asked.

"Uh-huh. It's all right, too, but it won't help any this month," Derwent said.

"I'm figuring strong on that hill. Don't let anybody move it away." Keegan grinned.

Derwent stared. He had no sense of humor, Keegan thought.

In the middle tent at Albo's, the only one open for business so early in the day, Keegan found a bartender he hadn't seen before. The man shook his head when Keegan inquired about Stroud. "I don't know him. I'm new here."

"He's in the tent next to mine," someone said.

Carson Albo was standing in the entrance, bare chest brown and glistening, his pale face damp with sweat under a wide-brimmed black hat.

"You want to hire him again?" Albo asked.

"Maybe. Why?"

Albo's smile was friendly. "I hate to see a good man go haywire, that's all. Work might straighten him out. Stroud's got a lot of good stuff in him to be acting the way he has." He walked unhurriedly up to the bar.

"Last night you weren't so interested in reforming men," Keegan said. "From what I saw neither were your barkeepers."

Albo's eyes darkened but his face was controlled. "Stroud is a little different. On top of that he owes me money — and on top of that McLean asked me to sort of look out for him."

"McLean?" Keegan's eyes narrowed.

Albo seemed to be enjoying himself. "McLean used to work for me when I was a contractor. In fact, he was with me when I went broke."

Keegan stared.

"Drink?" Albo asked; and then when Keegan shook his head, "You'll find Stroud in the tent next to mine."

Stroud was asleep in his clothes on a cot in the tent Keegan entered. The red-head didn't rouse easily, but when he finally swung to his feet over the edge of the bed and looked at Keegan his eyes showed recognition.

"When Liash comes back, Stroud, I don't want him to think I messed up his outfit any worse than I could help. How about coming back to work?"

Keegan sensed by the slow reaction on the battered, swollen face that the use of Liash Keegan's name had been the best approach he could have made, but after a while Stroud shook his head. "It won't work."

"Maybe not right now around camp," Keegan said. "But I'd like to have you go with Mike Uri and his partner hunting meat — right at first that is." He offered his hand. "I was lucky the first day we met."

Stroud hesitated and then shook hands, his bloodshot eyes and bruised face giving him an ugly, evil appearance.

When Keegan left fifteen minutes later Stroud had accepted the offer. He was going to borrow a horse and rifle from Albo and start for the hills that morning; among other duties he was going to keep an eye peeled for Branson.

As Keegan rode back to camp he tried to convince himself that he had made no mistake. Well, his father had trusted Stroud and McLean thought the red-head was all right.

Out of the morning's work the fact that McLean once had worked for Albo lay uppermost in Keegan's thoughts. But perhaps that fact meant no more than just what it appeared to mean. . . .

—CHAPTER FIFTEEN—

Tension coiled hard within Keegan as he lay on his cot and listened. Just before he had wakened he must have heard some sound, something that had warned him into consciousness, but there was no sound now and the tent was darker than doom.

His spine began to tingle and he contracted muscles to leap from the cot.

"You're a heavy sleeper, Keegan." The voice was Whisper Jim's, and he was standing almost beside the cot.

Keegan relaxed. "Do you ever get shot doing that?"

Whisper laughed dryly. "Not often." Keegan heard him sit down on a bale of hay. "I know who stampeded your herd."

Keegan sat up.

"They ain't important," Whisper said. "They was hired for the job, but I don't know yet who paid 'em. In time I'll find out."

"How?"

Whisper laughed gently. "Mostly I ride the other side of the fence, Keegan, but now and then I take up slack for a friend — like I'm doing now. In this case it's Capps."

Keegan thought fast. Capps had lost twenty thousand in a payroll holdup, and now perhaps Whisper Jim was on the trail of money — more likely the men, because the money probably hadn't stayed in anyone's pockets very long.

"That money they took from Capps has all been blown by now," Keegan said casually.

Whisper Jim was silent for several moments. "I think it hasn't. Only two men held up Capps, and two can keep their mouths shut better than five or six — and they can wait longer than a gang when it comes to dividing."

The thought opened the field wide for any and all of the men Keegan had discounted as suspects because he thought they lacked money.

"See if you can find out who was gone almost all night from camp the night Capps was robbed," Whisper said. "I know that'll be tough to find out, but try to anyway. I'll be by again before long."

"Yell out the next time."

Whisper laughed. "If you'd tie Bear Trap close to this tent no one but me could get in."

He went silently across the room. The tent flaps rasped softly on his buckskin jacket, and then the night took him.

Keegan lay awake for another hour. He had done part of his task: the work, thanks to Derwent, was going fairly well, but so thin was the partition between success and failure that one solid blow by whoever was against him would wreck the job and cost Liash Keegan his outfit.

In spite of many suspicions and a few facts, he was no closer to knowing who the troublemaker was than he had been the day he rode into camp. But when Laraine returned . . .

Sometime later when he leaped out of bed and felt for his boots there was no doubt as to what had waked him.

Someone had shot at least twice. He had his boots on and was pulling his gun from under his pillow when two more shots sounded, close to Grieve's tent, he estimated.

He ran into the night. Men were shouting questions in the bunk tents. The night guard at the yard was talking in an effort to soothe spooky horses. A lantern showed suddenly in Grieve's tent and Keegan went toward it.

The blacksmith was putting on his boots. He brushed the sole of one bare foot and grumbled to himself as Keegan stepped inside. "What happened?" Keegan asked.

"I don't know," Grieve said. "Some idiot was over by the graders. Just as I was going to sleep — I had a devil of a time going to sleep tonight — I heard him bump into something; sounded like he kicked against the plow. I took my rifle and went to the door. Just then he shot twice, so I up and shot twice at him."

"Was he shooting at you?" Keegan asked, puzzled.

"I don't know — but when some idiot starts shooting in the middle of the night you don't stop to ask him. I shot and he ran and that's all I know."

The blacksmith's dark hair was sticking on end; his eyes were heavy with dark pouches and he appeared to be disgusted with the whole evening. "I won't get to sleep at all now," he said. He looked sullenly at a rifle lying beside him on the cot, then went over to the stove and began to build a fire.

There was a light in McLean's quarters when Keegan went outside. Lanterns were bobbing around the camp and men were still yelling questions. Keegan went down to the storekeeper's tent.

"All right in there?" he yelled.

"Yeah!" McLean sounded angry. He came out a few moments later, half dressed. "What's going on?"

Men were crowding before the tent. Derwent was limping with one boot on, cursing someone who had stepped on his bare toes in the scramble from one of the bunk tents.

"Between drunks coming in from Albo's and people shooting around here, nobody gets any rest!" Derwent complained. "What was it now?"

Keegan felt McLean nudge him with one knee. "Some drunk shot in the air," Keegan said. "That made Grieve sore, so he took a shot or two on general principles."

If the feeble explanation fooled anyone it certainly wasn't Derwent, Keegan could see. Thinking about it, Keegan realized he had no explanation to give. "Grieve says the fellow was over by the elevating graders."

That brought a general surge of men and lanterns to the graders. The area had been well trampled daily by men going and coming from work and showed nothing to sustain or disprove Grieve's statement. By daylight there would be nothing to find around the graders, Keegan was sure.

He urged the crews back to bed. Derwent

160

speeded up the process, still grumbling about his injured toes.

When only McLean and Keegan were left in the cold night, the storekeeper said, "I'll show you something."

He led Keegan to dynamite stored beside the partition of baled hay in the commissary, set the lantern down carefully, and upended one of the boxes of dynamite closest to the front wall. The container showed a bullet hole in one end. There were two holes in the front of the tent, one about eighteen inches higher than the other and in line with a single hole in the back wall.

They opened the box. Gelatinous muck was mixed with sawdust where the bullet had coursed until stopped just short of completely penetrating the length of the box. Keegan recovered the lead.

He tapped one of the green-wrapped primer sticks. "If he'd hit one of those she might have blown. Though I've never heard of dynamite exploding from a shot, I still wouldn't want to experiment to prove it won't."

McLean glanced significantly at the baled hay. If the explosives had gone off, the finances of the Keegan Construction Company would have been scattered from hell to breakfast, not to mention McLean, the commissary, and close-lying tents.

"You can always beat the brains out of a gandy and make a storekeeper," McLean said. "But money comes hard."

Keegan wiped gelatin and sawdust off the slug. "What caliber would you say that was?"

"Maybe a forty-five."

Keegan studied the piece of lead. It could have come from a revolver, or it could have come from a rifle — specifically a rifle like Grieve's.

"That was pretty good shooting for as far away as those graders are," McLean said. "When you consider it was pitch dark."

"Uh-huh. But if a man sighted in when there was light by lining up with braces or part of the frame on one of those graders, he could have walked over there in the dark and rested his gun right where he'd lined it up before."

McLean stared thoughtfully and nodded.

The incident, Keegan thought, had done at least one good thing: it had eliminated McLean as a suspect. Forthwith Keegan told him of Laraine's mission with the Prairie Giant; of Boxcar Branson and of Whisper Jim's visit.

"It looks like Branson can give us some answers." McLean's eyes held a cold glitter.

Dawn was breaking when Keegan went back to his own quarters and dressed fully. He took his time and considered the night's shooting in relation to every man he had suspected. If Grieve had been telling the truth about seeing someone standing near McLean's tent the night Keegan had made the slip in mentioning the payroll, that eavesdropper wouldn't have to be very smart to know that the gold was most probably concealed in McLean's quarters.

Then Stroud might have known it was there and he might have told others, including Albo.

Of course the attempt might have been no more than an effort to wreck the camp. The gold could stay where it was, Keegan thought, but the explosives would be moved at daylight and put under guard.

He went over the events from the time the first shots had brought him out of sleep. It had taken him some time to find his boots and put them on. Grieve could have fired all four shots, the last two as he ran back to his tent.

Derwent could have been the man by the

grader, joining sleep-groggy men as they ran from the bunk tents, with none of them even aware that he hadn't been in his bunk when the first shots came. His bunk was the first one inside the door of one of the sleeping quarters. He had had a gun in his hand when Keegan met him near the commissary, but so had several of the others.

Only McLean seemed to be in the clear. Keegan paused suddenly in the act of buttoning his shirt. Was McLean in the clear? He could have fired the two shots from the grader and then run to his quarters when Grieve shot. There was no way of telling whether or not the gold had even been in its hiding place during the excitement.

McLean might have carried it some distance away and then tried to blow up the tent. Keegan considered going back to the storekeeper's quarters and taking a look; but sufficient time had passed now to have given McLean a chance to put the sacks back in their place — even if he had moved them.

I trusted Stroud because people told me my father trusted him, Keegan thought. Now why should I go out of my way to suspect McLean — the one man Liash said I could trust?

He finished dressing and went out to look at the graders.

As he had theorized, there were a dozen or more metal angles where a rested gun would point directly at the side of the commissary where the dynamite was.

In the late afternoon Laraine Grieve drove into camp behind the team of black geldings. Keegan saw her from a cut where he was supervising drillers, but he had no opportunity to talk to her until dusk when they met near the elevating graders.

Just looking at her made him realize that he had missed her, even though he had been strenuously occupied. This darkhaired girl with the slow, provocative smile was getting into his life a little deeper each time he thought about her.

If he pulled the outfit out of its hole and moved on west . . . But if he didn't make the riffle . . .

"What are you thinking about?" she asked.

"The gun I gave you," he said quickly.

She smiled. "That track worker was young once. He talked to me like he thought he still was."

Keegan asked a question with his eyes.

She nodded. "The man who killed your friend was standing awful close to him —

165

and the gun he used had a staghorn grip."

"Prairie Giant?" Keegan asked.

She nodded slowly.

"Anything else?"

"He wasn't a very large man. The old fellow said he was wrinkled like dry leather and had a big brown face with a hammer jaw and a big nose."

"That's the fellow!" Keegan said.

"Do you know him?"

"I will," Keegan said grimly.

—CHAPTER SIXTEEN—

Riding to the hills to seek Branson, McLean said, would be courageous, heroic and altogether foolish. He pointed out that the day Keegan had made inquiries about Branson a dozen men had heard him.

"If Branson is the man who can lead us to the root of the trouble, you can bet he's been warned by now," McLean said. "He's up there with the payroll crowd, and they wouldn't be likely to stand by chewing their cud while you rode up and tried to force the truth out of Boxcar."

There was a good deal of truth in McLean's opinion, Keegan admitted, but still he wanted Boxcar Branson. "I think I'll go after him anyway."

"Wait till after payday and I'll go with you," McLean said. He studied Keegan. "I'd suggest, though, that you wait till Stroud and the others come down again. Maybe they'll know something; and another thing: Branson may wander into Albo's any time. He likes to gamble."

In the end Keegan decided to follow

McLean's advice. He walked to the grade each day, giving particular attention to the rock work, one field where he was completely sure of himself.

As payday drew closer he noticed increasing nervousness among some of the crews, a growing sullenness in others. They were worried about their money and knew he hadn't been out of camp to bring in the payroll. A few men quit and were paid off. Keegan assured the rest that they would get their wages when the time came.

Then from somewhere the rumor started that Laraine had brought in the money; the story grew and became accepted as solid truth, and Keegan received congratulations from some for employing such a clever ruse to fool hold-up men. Even Derwent asked in all seriousness if the yarn were true.

Keegan did not deny it. Laraine discredited the story with a smile that made her listeners sure that she had brought the payroll. The work resumed its normal pace and everyone felt assured of at least one more payday before Keegan Construction Company gave up the ghost.

Albo was not pleased with the story. He spoke coldly to Keegan about it in the gambling tent, nightly haunted by the latter on the lookout for Branson.

"I hear you're letting women take your risks," Albo said.

"You can hear anything if you let your ears hang," Keegan said.

Albo's nostrils tightened. His eyes darkened and he watched Keegan quietly, the latter wondering if Albo's worry was caused entirely by interest in Laraine. "If you *did* let her do that," Albo said, "it was a cowardly trick."

"If she did do it — that was her business."

They measured each other quietly.

"No, I don't believe you'd let her take a chance like that," Albo said, and walked away to watch a poker game.

Keegan stood at the bar watching the broad-shouldered man move from table to table until he reached the wheel-of-fortune. Albo never gambled himself, Keegan had noticed, and though he watched his gamblers carefully, Albo didn't appear to have genuine interest in the business he was conducting.

Just how far Laraine had influenced Albo toward giving up whisky and gambling was something that worried Keegan more than he cared to admit, for the measure of Laraine's success might also be the measure of her interest in Albo.

The saloonman still rode to the edge of Keegan's camp at least twice a week, and Laraine always went out to talk to him, while Grieve stood glowering at them from the front of his tent. Along with other things he had to settle, Keegan thought he'd better include an understanding with Laraine, even if the doing forced a showdown with Albo.

He ordered a drink and watched the crowd. Play was unusually heavy tonight, since Capps had paid a portion of his crew that had completed their work. They were celebrating before heading on west, where Capps already had sent part of his equipment.

Keegan watched Albo congratulate a lean freighter who had just made a killing on the wheel-of-fortune.

Albo seemed to be genuinely happy about the man's good luck, and as Keegan watched he thought that it wouldn't be difficult to be friends with the saloonman, even if he did vaguely suspect Albo of being connected with the trouble besetting Keegan Construction Company.

He studied the crowd, making sure that Branson had not come in while he was engrossed with Albo. Boxcar Branson was not in the room. Keegan went to the next tent.

He was loitering by a table when Penrose Capps entered, pushing his way down the crowded room with little regard for men's balance or bodies. Some cursed him after he had passed, but they gave way while he was passing.

Keegan noticed that Capps was wearing the same outsize pants he had had on almost a month before. The wrinkles in front had caught a little more dust; his Scotch cap was a little darker around the edges that fitted on the head, and Capps' hair was a great deal longer around his ears.

He spoke to Keegan and nodded toward the bar. "Have one?"

Keegan stepped forward and Capps made room for two men at the bar by sheer weight. The burly construction company owner tossed off his whisky without bothering to remove his snuff. The half-smile came to his lips.

"I hear you're shooting day and night down on your end of the job," Capps said.

Keegan grinned. "We try to keep busy." He studied Capps. "Whisper doing you any good?"

Capps' face was expressionless, his little eyes hard and quiet. "Maybe. Before you get through with Whisper you pay plenty."

Keegan was pondering over that remark

and about to ask a direct question when he saw Capps' attention veer suddenly toward the entrance.

Grieve was just inside the tent.

"Mind if I try to hire your blacksmith — again?" Capps' faint smile moved the corners of his mouth. He didn't wait for an answer, but went lumbering and shoving his way toward Grieve, and the two men went outside together.

A good construction blacksmith was hard to find, Keegan considered thoughtfully, and it was Capps' way to go hard after something he wanted without regard for others — but still Keegan wondered if Capps and Grieve had other business between them in addition to blacksmithing.

Branson, a man Keegan had seen exactly once, was still the best route to finding out a lot of answers. Keegan decided that he would wait one more night for Branson and then go after him, whether McLean or anyone else considered the move foolhardy.

At midnight he went back to camp. He had followed Whisper Jim's advice and tethered Bear Trap close to the tent. The mule's big ears and ugly head loomed out of the darkness, but after a wrinkling of big teeth Bear Trap decided to pass Keegan.

"Do whatever you want," McLean said

172

the next morning. "But I'd say wait till tomorrow night at least. Tomorrow's payday for us and Capps too. There'll be plenty of loose money at Albo's that night, and like I said, Branson is a sucker for gambling. Besides, Stroud and the others are due in tomorrow and they may have a line on him."

They were washing on the bench by the water tank. On the other side of the tank Long Neck Wilson was working the handle of a force pump to transfer a load of water he had brought in the night before. The bunk tents were just coming to life, Derwent roaring at men to get up.

Long Neck Wilson, who had been muttering at the faulty operation of his pump, suddenly cut loose with full-force profanity. They heard him pulling the hose out of his tank wagon, still cursing.

For the second time Keegan decided to follow McLean's advice. He knew it was not inspired by fear: along with his cold-bloodedness McLean was well steeped in common sense.

They went around the tank to see the teamster beating the intake end of the hose against the wagon. The end of the hose was choked, and as they watched the stoppage came free.

Keegan's stomach almost turned at what dropped on the ground. Pieces from the body of a rattlesnake had been blocking the hose.

"Hell's fire and a bucket of mud," Long Neck said.

Men just arriving at the washbench came around the tent and stared. One of them began to retch.

"I don't want to drink any water hauled in that tank — ever!" someone said. His opinion was general.

The water went on the ground.

After breakfast Keegan rode toward the railhead water tank on the Yankee Falls side of Coyote Hill. The night raid, the attempt to blow up the camp — nothing had ever filled him with the cold, deadly anger he felt now.

According to Long Neck's account, he had filled his tank on the last trip and then had retired to the shady side of a wagon with other teamsters for ten or fifteen minutes of talk. Five or six men, to whom no one had paid any particular attention, had ridden past while the skinners were having their gabfest.

Long Neck said he hadn't recognized any of the riders, but Keegan knew that one of them had known Wilson's outfit.

The railhead tank was the only possible place where the water could have been found, because no one had come close to Long Neck on his trip, and the wagon had been under guard almost from the instant it reached camp.

Keegan had been thankful for Wilson's vehement assurance that the snake fragments hadn't been in the wagon tank from any previous trips, since Long Neck swore he had flushed the tank just before filling it the last time.

An hour passed before Keegan saw the first water-hauler approaching.

The teamster was a bulky, squat extrovert wearing a wide studded belt; he said the studs were made of a special metal that was a safeguard against rheumatism.

"You remember the five or six men that rode by last night just when you fellows were ready to pull out?" Keegan asked. "Or were you here then?"

"I made as many trips as anybody."

"Did you know any of the men?" Keegan asked.

The teamster squinted curiously. "I knew one of 'em, a fellow that plays a lot of stud at Albo's — poorest poker player you ever saw. I remember one night —"

"What's his name?"

The skinner thought. "Blanding — Brandon — anyway, I always just called him Boxcar."

"Big jaw, nose like a ham, brown face — ?"

"Yeah!" The teamster nodded happily. "That's him! I remember one night when he had the joker in the hole —"

Keegan didn't hear the rest of the story. He was riding away. He considered checking in Capps' camp to find out if anyone there had seen Branson, but decided that would arouse too much interest; the voluble teamster would no doubt do plenty of talking as it was, but there was no need to give Branson any more warning than could be helped.

Keegan reflected that every effort he had made to pin down facts had failed, except for his theory about Branson.

He had tried to find out where everybody had been the night Capps was robbed, and the facts had become very slippery in the process. Stroud and McLean had been in Yankee Falls ordering supplies. Laraine had ridden there with them, but she hadn't seen them after parting on arrival.

Derwent said he had been visiting in Capps' camp. Grieve claimed to have been at Albo's in the company of two of Liash Keegan's teamsters who since had been fired. Keegan hadn't asked Albo, but McLean said the saloonman had been away on a two-day hunting trip.

Again that night Keegan prowled Albo's until late, but Branson did not show up. The next day he helped McLean pay the men after the end of shift, and they streamed toward the whisky tents while still chewing their suppers.

An hour later Stroud and the other two meat hunters drove into camp. The huge redhead was clear-eyed and clean-shaven. For the first time Keegan recognized in him some of the qualities, other than a resemblance to a boy killed in the Civil War, that must have attracted old Liash Keegan.

Stroud glanced at Keegan significantly and then strolled beyond the water tank where soap scum showed on the rocks from efforts to cleanse Long Neck's water tank.

"The other day I stopped for a drink in one of the payroll crowd's camp," Stroud said. "Boxcar is supposed to meet someone at Albo's tonight."

—CHAPTER SEVENTEEN—

McLean, Stroud and Keegan rode toward Albo's. Derwent had already gone to the gambling and whisky tents, Keegan had found out, and Grieve had been left behind in camp to watch McLean's quarters, the detail having been explained to Grieve as a precaution against tampering with the time-books as well as a necessary move to guard against pilfering of the commissary.

"Of all the nights the commissary ought to be open, this is it," McLean complained. "Tomorrow everybody will be busted and wanting to buy clothes on tick. Every payday is the same."

Keegan was not greatly interested in petty finances at the moment. His brain was fondling the thought that at last he was about to get a solid grip on Boxcar Branson, and hereby, he hoped, on the elusive trouble he hadn't been able to cope with.

"We'll each take one tent," he said. "Don't make a move toward him if you see him before I do. Just let me know."

"I don't know what it's all about," Stroud said. "But I never did like that slope-headed Branson. He tried to knife me once in an argument when I was a foreman."

At one end of Albo's camp they ground-hitched their mounts and made a final check of guns.

Stroud and McLean walked away to begin their vigil and Keegan went toward the nearest of the three main tents. He stopped after a few steps when he heard the familiar snap of Bear Trap's teeth.

With one hand on the gun in his pocket, he walked back toward the mounts. Someone was standing close to the mule. Keegan heard a gentle laugh.

"He still knows me," came the voice of Whisper Jim. He laughed again. "Who are you about to hang?"

Keegan walked close to the tall, buck-skin-clad man. "I didn't think we looked that determined," he said. He tried to study Whisper's face, thinking that only once had he seen the man in daylight. "I couldn't get any satisfaction when I tried to find out where my top men were the night Capps was robbed."

"Well, it never hurts to try," Whisper said. "I couldn't find out a great deal myself, but

I picked up the trail of one man."

Keegan looked toward the tents. Stroud already had disappeared in the middle one and McLean was just going through the doorway of another. Then Penrose Capps appeared in the light streaming from the far shelter and came stumping toward the middle tent and went inside.

Whisper's throaty laugh was mirthless. "Our stand, I'd say, was this nearest tent."

Men whose gold was heavy and hot in their pockets were bulging the walls of the tent Keegan and Whisper entered.

Keegan marveled at the way Whisper made his way to the crowded bar, cleaving a path that was easy to follow. Somehow men seemed to fall aside to make passage as soon as they glanced at Whisper's ice-blue eyes.

The man in buckskin declined a drink. He stood with his back to the bar and searched the room with alert movements of his cold eyes.

Struck by a sudden hunch, Keegan said, "We might be looking for the same man."

"We might."

"I want him alive," Keegan said.

Whisper's eyes left the crowd for just an instant as he looked at Keegan. "So do I."

They waited.

Poker games flourished, men standing two-deep behind the players while waiting for an empty chair. Drinkers came and went at the bar and the spigoted whisky barrels scarcely stopped flowing a moment. Men pushed back their chairs at the tables, rose and left, and others leaped to take their places.

"Did I tell you I'm pretty sure the gang that tried to rob Liash wasn't connected in any way with your troubles?" Whisper asked.

"No, but I've been thinking that myself." Whisper Jim, Keegan thought, must be solid with the payroll crowd, getting his information as one outlaw would tell another. There was a great deal about Whisper that he didn't know, and as he thought about it he concluded that he never would know but a few details about the man.

Keegan's eyes narrowed when he saw Grieve step into the tent and look around as if trying to find someone. The black-smith should have been in camp guarding McLean's quarters where a few thousand in gold still lay.

Grieve saw Keegan, nodded, and then went out a few moments later, apparently not finding the man he wanted.

The smith scarcely had left when a terrific uproar broke out in the next tent. Voices raised in anger, shouting, cursing. Someone yelled, "Outside! Get 'em outside!"

A gun shot sounded.

Men around Whisper and Keegan stampeded to see the excitement. Someone overturned a poker table. Drunks shouted with laughter and a dealer cursed.

"The back way," Whisper Jim said calmly.

Keegan followed him around the bar and out the rear entrance. He thought he was right behind him when they started around the corner of the tent, but Keegan felt nobody ahead of him when he tripped over tent ropes and fell against an empty barrel with his shoulder.

Judging from the yells in front of the tents, everybody was fighting. Another gunshot rose heavy and hard above the uproar of voices.

When Keegan reached the scene he looked over heads to see four or five men fighting in the uncertain light of lanterns waved by wobbly spectators.

Then someone yelled, "Here's a man shot!"

Others took up the shout. Still others began to bellow questions.

Lantern bearers left fighting men to do the best they could and went toward the center of the excited shouting.

Keegan fought his way without respect for the individual dignity of man. He left a wake of cursing men and reached the focal point of excitement just behind a lantern bearer.

Whisper Jim was kneeling on the ground beside a man whose face was ghastly in the yellow light, whose eyes were wide with shock.

The man was Boxcar Branson.

His wide lips moved close to Whisper's ear, and then his eyes rolled a little. They fixed on someone in the ring of men above him and filled with dark hatred. And then they lost all expression but an eerie stare.

Keegan glanced where Branson's eyes had seen someone whose face had stirred the dying man to hatred.

Albo and Stroud were standing close together where Keegan looked; he knew none of the other men close to them.

Whisper Jim stood up. "He got it right in the back."

The crowd was silent for a moment, and then it began to break up, some moving back to talk in little knots, others crowding forward to look briefly at the dead man, and others going back inside the tents to resume their interrupted revel.

Two men were still fighting, locked and rolling on the ground. Only their friends paid them any attention.

Keegan found himself the center of a little group of his own men, all trying to talk at once. He cursed savagely. "Let's hear one at a time!"

"I was just inside the middle tent," Grieve said. "I was looking for Capps. Just as I seen him at the bar this ruckus started and carried me right out of the tent. I didn't even notice Boxcar."

"He'd come in just ahead of you," Derwent said. "I saw him."

"That's right!" Stroud nodded vigorously. "I saw Boxcar start toward the bar — me and Capps was standing almost together — and then the brawl broke loose at a poker table. By the time I got out of the tent, I'd lost track of everybody."

Keegan couldn't do anything but rage helplessly to himself. He told his own experience and realized it was no more help than any he'd heard so far.

McLean's cool voice cut in at the finish. "Boxcar was looking for somebody. I seen him take a gander around the end tent where I was. When he went out I followed to keep an eye on him. I saw him go in the middle tent, then Grieve. When the trouble began I saw Grieve jump to get in the clear, but so many men came out at once after that I couldn't tell one from another."

Somebody, Keegan knew, had walked or run right behind Boxcar during the confusion, shooting him with little risk of detection. "Let's see your guns," he said bluntly.

The request was a dangerous one and Keegan knew it, but he was in no mood to weigh danger at the moment and was cursing himself for not having ridden to the hills after Boxcar several days before.

For a while the dead silence of the four men was weighted with refusal.

Then McLean said, "That's a mighty big request, but reasonable, considering everything." He passed his double-barreled Remington derringer to Keegan.

Men watched curiously as Keegan knelt by the lantern sitting near the dead man and examined the bores of four guns.

Three of the weapons were clean. Grieve's was dusty in the barrel and appeared not to have been fired for years.

As Keegan stood up he saw Albo among the curious watchers. The tall saloonman's mouth twitched a little with amusement as he lit a cigar. He blew a cloud of smoke toward the stars and walked away.

Some of Stroud's belligerence bubbled up. "Now let's see yours, Keegan."

Without a word Keegan passed the gun to the redhead, who knelt by the lantern and examined it. "Clean," he said, looking at the others. "Anybody want to see it?"

No one did.

Stroud stood up, grinning. "That makes us all even."

And exactly where we started, Keegan thought.

Grieve yawned. "Anybody going back to camp? I told Laraine I wouldn't be gone long. I left her to look after Mac's precious papers."

"Why didn't you say you weren't going to stay when Keegan asked you?" McLean demanded.

"I remembered afterward that I promised to tell Capps what I'd decided about him offering to hire me," Grieve said. He looked at Keegan. "I decided to stay with the outfit."

The blacksmith walked off into the darkness. Keegan went in search of Carson Albo. He found him in the middle tent talking to Whisper Jim. Business had resumed in full force and a few more fights were in the making.

Whisper's cold eyes were on Albo, but he spoke to Keegan. "Albo tells me Boxcar spent last night here."

There was no strain in Albo's voice. "Sure he did! I've seen him around here several times, but I didn't know his name. He came riding in about dark, said he'd been in the saddle for forty hours and was dog-tired. You can't refuse a sober man a bed."

All the time he'd been waiting last night for Boxcar, Keegan thought, the man had been only fifty feet away in the tent next to Albo's.

"What did he have to say last night?" Keegan asked.

"He said he was going to meet somebody here tonight."

"He did," Whisper said tonelessly.

—CHAPTER EIGHTEEN—

Two more weeks of brutal work under a hot sun served to drive home to Keegan the hard fact that nothing short of a miracle could make the job meet the next payroll. The miracle could lie in the hill his crews were nearing, but common sense told him that loose material was not going to run all the way to the bottom of the cut that had to be made.

Track crews were crowding Capps hard. They caught him short at the east end of his work and engineers penalized him for delaying the rails, a loss which Capps' men declared was immediately recovered by reducing rations.

It wouldn't be long before the track layers would be crowding Keegan. Except for the hill he had saved as an ace in the hole, his grade was nearly finished, but he needed the yardage of the hill and all the rest he could make to realize enough on estimates to carry the outfit.

Four days would get him to the hill; a week, he estimated, would be enough to make the cut. And then he had to get a final estimate from the engineers, make the long trip to Ogden to collect from the railroad's disbursing agent, and get back to pay the men.

If he could delay payday a few days he might barely have enough time — if he could move the hill in a week.

There were too many "ifs" in that plan to risk losing Liash Keegan's outfit. Borrowing money was the safe play — and that had a large "if" in it also.

He stood watching the crews stringing toward the grade to start the day's work. Two Irish laborers stopped to light their pipes. "Another day toward the million we'll be making," one said.

Their laughter was bright in the cool early-morning air.

A dump cart jounced by with sharp steel for the morning's drilling. Two strapping hammermen went past, grinning like boys as they balanced their seven-pound double-packs with the ends of the handles on one finger.

"The wind blew and the dust flew, and where'll we be in a month or two!" one chanted.

In spite of his worries Keegan laughed. He was still grinning when Laraine came up beside him. "You like it, don't you?" she asked.

"Sure I like it!"

"You *are* going west when this is done, aren't you?"

He laughed. "I may start *before* it's done."

"I want to go on too." She gave him a long, level look, and he realized that it was the time to speak some of the thoughts in his mind. But until the job was done, until he pulled the outfit into the clear . . .

"It's a hard life for —"

"You said that before." She smiled as he walked away.

If McLean was worried he showed no trace of it when he and Keegan discussed their problems in the commissary a half-hour later.

"You'll have to borrow money," McLean said. "The bank in Yankee Falls is well fixed, but I hear Rowden, the banker, is tighter — well, you've heard the story of the Jersey bull in fly season."

Keegan nodded. He knew that finances were running low, with just little more left than enough to meet current expenses. "I'll try tomorrow," Keegan said.

Before sunrise next morning he was riding out of camp. He was less than half the distance to Albo's when Laraine overtook him on one of the stocky black geldings she used on the spring wagon.

Twice before he had seen a woman wearing men's pants: a huge miner panning gold in Montana beside her four strapping sons; and a woman who drove a wagon for Sheridan's headquarters company for three months before being detected.

Laraine looked like neither. "Where are *you* going?" Keegan asked.

She smiled. "I have business in Yankee Falls. If you don't want to ride with me —"

He laughed.

Albo caught up with them before they reached Capps' camp. His saddle bags, Keegan noticed, were bulging. Albo's smile was friendly, a trifle too friendly, Keegan thought, when it flashed toward Laraine.

"Mind if I ride along?" Albo asked, looking at Keegan.

"We'll be glad to have you," Laraine said.

"Yeah." Keegan had to laugh at himself when Laraine's laugh rang out, but a moment later he was thinking that Boxcar's last conscious expression had been directed at Carson Albo — or Stroud.

Perhaps the dying Branson, seeing Stroud, a man with whom he'd fought once, had reacted from the memory of that trouble — but maybe he'd looked at Albo as a betrayer, as the man who had shot him in the back.

Keegan had a dead-sure hunch that the

person who had killed Branson was the same man Boxcar was to have met, and the same man who was trying to hamstring the Keegan Construction Company.

Albo spoke as though reading Keegan's mind. "Did your buckskin chum show you the gun he picked up by Boxcar Branson's body the night Branson got killed?"

Keegan's eyes were hard and questioning.

"He picked up a cap and ball pistol like a dealer palms an ace," Albo said. "I saw him, and a little later I saw him give the gun back to Capps." Albo smiled. "That's why I was grinning when I saw you checking the guns of your men."

The words had the ring of truth. Either that or a great lie carelessly told by a master liar, Keegan wasn't sure which. "Gave it *back* to Capps?" he asked.

"He gave it to Capps, and I've seen Capps carry a cap and ball pistol now and then that looked a whole lot like the same gun." Albo grinned. "But I wouldn't swear to that in court."

The hooves of the horses raked lava rock for fifty yards before anyone spoke.

"Maybe someone snatched the gun out of Capps' pocket," Laraine said. "It doesn't sound likely that a man would leave his revolver right where he'd killed another man."

That was something he hadn't thought of, Keegan told himself, wondering if his readiness to grasp the thought was motivated more by unwillingness to think that he had been fooled by Whisper Jim than by sound logic. Still it was quite possible that someone could have taken Capps' gun from his pocket, considering the way men had been crowded against each other, surging, and rushing to get outside the tents.

In spite of himself he began to believe that Albo had told the truth.

"Suppose you try to spend just one day without scowling over your problems," Laraine said.

The suggestion was good, Keegan admitted — but hard to follow. Nevertheless, before the ride was over he was not finding it difficult to forget temporarily some of his problems. He found Albo a genial companion and thought again that here was a man with whom he could quite easily be friendly.

They watered their horses at the Snake in midafternoon and rode into the town, parting with Laraine before a frame house where an enormous woman surrounded by children welcomed Laraine heartily and regarded the two men suspiciously even after they were introduced.

Albo tipped his hat politely. "I'll be getting on to the bank," he said.

Keegan rode with him as far as a red livery stable, stopping to leave Bear Trap. Albo hesitated before going on.

"This is my last stand in the saloon and gambling business," he said. "I'm going back to contracting."

Keegan looked at Albo's bulging saddle bags, and the latter nodded. "Yes, I've done well enough." He watched Keegan steadily for a moment and then rode away.

Fifteen minutes later, in a bank building next to a grocery store, Keegan found Penrose Capps waiting ahead of him to see Banker Rowden. Albo's empty saddle bags lay on a chair next to Capps. From an office at the back of the room Keegan heard a murmur of voices and then Albo's clear laugh.

Capps' little eyes gleamed with humor. "How many times did you walk up and down the street before you got up nerve to come in?"

Keegan grinned. "I thought this was a saloon. I made it in one try."

A lean, pinch-faced teller scowled in disapproval.

"I hear you lost your gun the other

night," Keegan said casually, watching Capps keenly.

Capps' eyes lost their humor instantly. "Uh huh. Somebody grabbed it out of my coat during that free-for-all."

They stared at each other, Keegan thinking that there was no way of telling if Capps had told the truth — except that the man had been blunt and straightforward previously.

Albo came out of the private office, followed to the door by a small, brisk man whose eyes swept quickly over Keegan and Capps even while the banker was shaking hands with Albo.

A few moments later Keegan felt himself beginning to sweat as he waited alone, listening to the heavy rumble of Capps' voice in the private office. It seemed to Keegan that the clean-clothed, clean-handed tellers were watching him with mingled pity and disgust.

Capps stumped heavily out of the office five minutes later, his face set in bleak, hard lines. Sure as the world, Keegan thought, he's tried for a loan and missed.

Rowden smiled at Keegan and said, "Come in, sir."

Keegan watched Capps' broad back move through the street door. A tiny, vague warning that he couldn't pin down started to nag in Keegan's brain.

"Come in, sir!" Rowden said.

Once seated in the banker's office, Keegan found Rowden friendly as well as brisk. The little man listened carefully to Keegan's request, his sharp eyes probing, weighing.

"I've heard of your work and your — ah — difficulties too, Mr. Keegan," Rowden said. "Personally, I consider you a sound investment, but of course I have associates and investors to protect. Give me three days for necessary inquiries."

"Three days!"

Rowden nodded briskly. "Yes, it will take that long at least to check your father's credit in Omaha, and — well, his condition at the moment will have some bearing." Rowden's smile was quick and friendly. "Come back on the morning of the fourth day."

The next three days seemed the longest Keegan had ever spent. On the morning of the fourth he stood in a saloon across the street and waited until he saw Rowden enter the bank.

The banker was brief. "Your father is making a remarkable recovery. I know you'll be glad to know that." He hesitated.

"But I'm sorry to say that we can't make the loan. Matters involved with the financing of the railroad in the East have led us to believe . . ."

Keegan didn't hear the rest. He was thinking of Albo, wondering if the saloonman had dropped remarks or made hints when he was talking to Rowden. Still, the banker had wired for information.

"I'm genuinely sorry, Mr. Keegan."

Keegan mustered a grin as he rose. "So am I."

Grimly he thought that he would have to produce a miracle from the hill he had saved to the last. Some way.

As he crossed the street on his way to the livery stable he thought he saw a flash of a tall buckskin-clad figure moving away from the saloon window where he himself had watched for Rowden. If it *was* Whisper Jim or the devil himself, Keegan had no time to waste at the moment.

Absorbed in thoughts about the hill he had to move in less than record time, he rode squarely into a holdup staged by five masked men where the train ran through a rock jumble less than ten miles from Yankee Falls.

One dismounted man stepped out in front of him. Three covered him with rifles from the rocks; and one came almost noiselessly behind him. He dismounted and submitted to their inspection.

The man who walked up from the front and searched Keegan had no trouble with Bear Trap, though the mule snapped at him playfully. Bear Trap was not so playful with the man behind, who started to examine the McClellan saddle; just by a fraction the mule failed to mangle the fellow's wrist.

Keegan lost nothing. The tall man in front gave him back his unloaded gun and said, "Ride!" His voice was a throaty whisper, his eyes ice-blue above the mask, and his buckskin jacket was dark and shiny from long wear.

As Keegan rode away he tried to recall one of Capps' incomplete statements . . . "Whisper Jim costs plenty before you're through with him. . . ."

—CHAPTER NINETEEN—

Keegan didn't hurry the rest of his trip. He wanted to get in well after dark so that no more men than necessary would know that he was returning empty-handed.

McLean, Derwent and Grieve were in the storekeeper's quarters when Keegan pushed past the flaps. They were sitting in silence and they looked at Keegan without speaking. One of Derwent's eyes was closed; his upper lip was fat and his face was angry with lumps and bruises.

"Capps moved in on our hill three days ago," McLean said. "Derwent tackled him about it and they had a little trouble."

"How can he make *that* stick?" Keegan's voice was calmer than he thought possible.

"He can make it stick by holding it and doing the work," Grieve said wearily. "He sent more of his outfit west a few days ago, but he's still got twice the men we have."

McLean nodded. "The railroad people don't care who builds grade. They pay the ones who do the work."

"We can tackle his damned camp for

him!" Derwent said savagely. "Even if he has got twice the men!"

"That's the way I feel," Keegan said. "But a pitched battle would ruin us if we won." Capps, he thought, probably had gambled on the same knowledge.

They heard the crunch of boots outside and Stroud hailed the tent. "Come on, Mac, and weigh your blasted meat!"

Stroud's big shoulders plowed aside the tent flaps. He straightened and looked around the crowded room. "Liash — did Liash — ?"

Keegan explained briefly.

"Why, I stopped to look at that cut tonight on the way in," Stroud said. "I thought our own outfit —"

"There wasn't anyone there?" Keegan asked quickly.

Stroud shook his head. "Not a soul!"

Keegan grinned. "Here's what we'll do. . . ."

When the rays of the sun began to warm rattlesnakes in the cut behind him, Keegan was sitting on a mass of lava rock watching men approaching from Capps' camp. On his right, behind the hill, sat Long Neck Wilson's tank wagon near the mess tent. Men's blankets and other gear were piled on the ground nearby.

Behind him on the hill overlooking the cut was his full force, some sleeping after their night's work, all lying prone and out of sight. More than half of them had guns. Keegan himself was armed.

If Capps wanted a battle it was here for him. That he had sent a large part of his outfit west was an indication that he wasn't as broke as Keegan, unless he was taking a long gamble. In that case he might fight. Keegan knew he had to hold the hill and work it, slim as the chance was of making it pay off in time to meet his obligations.

The first teams passed Albo's and neared the pile of Capps' equipment moved the night before. The teamsters stared curiously at the lone figure on the rock.

"Hitch on and drag it back to Capps!" Keegan yelled at the teamsters. "He's through working here!"

"Who says so?" Two of the drivers walked forward until they recognized Keegan. They detoured around him and peered suspiciously into the cut. They looked at the silent hill above and went back to their companions.

One of them mounted a horse and went, harness flapping, toward the stream of men coming from Capps' camp. The stream piled up around the messenger; then it moved forward, and Capps emerged, bumping along on an enormous work horse. He looked at the hill behind Keegan and told his men to stay back.

Capps dismounted heavily before the man on the rock, and Keegan noted bruises that proved Derwent had put up a stiff fight.

"I should've expected this," Capps said.

Keegan watched him without speaking.

"I need this," Capps said. "Didn't get my loan."

"Neither did I."

They measured each other, Keegan relaxed outside, tense as a coiled spring inside. Capps worked his stubbled lower jaw against the lump of snuff behind his lower lip and studied Keegan. Then he raised his eyes to the hill.

"All your boys there?" he asked.

Keegan grinned.

"Guess I'll have to take it then." Capps made a slow, hooking gesture with one arm and his men started forward.

Alert as he was, Keegan didn't entirely avoid the blow that was a powerful follow-through of Capps' deliberate signal. Capps's fist raked along Keegan's jaw and helped turn Keegan's quick side leap into a near fall. Capps almost fell from the momentum of his own swing.

Keegan recovered balance and grounded his feet into loose waste to get solid footing. He heard shouting on the hill, shouting from Capps' men. A rifle shot sounded above the cut.

Capps came in slowly, thick arms bent, shoulders hunched. At close quarters the man would be murderous, Keegan thought.

Dynamite exploded in the cut, sending whistling sand and small fragments past Keegan's head. Stroud, he knew, had tossed down a short-fused stick to show Capps' men that the hill was held by more than guns.

Keegan tried Capps' jaw twice, both solid, straight punches. Capps weaved his head slowly and came on. Too late Keegan tried to step back. Capps' blows were club-like. They knocked down Keegan's guard with bruising power. And then the side of Capps' clenched hand struck Keegan's neck and sent him sprawling.

He rolled just in time to avoid Capps' boots as they came down close together after a short jump that had been calculated to end on Keegan's stomach.

The sweeping blow that Keegan

launched even before he was fully on his feet was a wild swing that would have netted him a disabled elbow had he been against a boxer. Capps was no boxer. He started a roundhouse of his own.

Keegan's fist caught Capps in the pit of the stomach, and then Keegan knew where paydirt lay when Capps grunted in pain. Keegan's arms were bruised from fending clubbing blows before he got two more solid jolts into Capps' stomach.

And then he landed a clincher that brought a hoarse groan from Capps. The burly man sat down, mouth working for air. He showed no ability to rise immediately.

Keegan glanced around. The whole hill was covered with shouting men, some waving guns. Capps' crew was standing silent and waiting.

After a time Capps rose slowly. His eyes still held fight, but they had another expression, too — the look of a man who knows his body won't carry him farther.

"I heard you was a belly puncher," he grunted. He stood hunched over, looking steadily at Keegan. Then he said, "Keep your damned hill." He turned and lumbered back to his men.

If I keep this hill, Keegan thought, *it will only be through force.*

Capps took his men away while Keegan's crews leaped up and down on the hill and jeered. They didn't celebrate long: Derwent put them to work. He told Keegan that the one shot on the hill had been an attempt by Derwent to shoot Capps, and that Grieve had knocked the rifle up.

"It's a lucky thing I didn't shoot him," Derwent said. "Rough as that old rascal is, some of his men think pretty well of him, but I was so sore I didn't care much at the time."

Two days and nights Keegan held the ground. He worked his crews in two twelve-hour shifts, Stroud taking the swing, and Derwent bossing the day shift. Men toiled by lantern light, and when kerosene began to run low Stroud made crude lamps of pans, rags, and bacon grease.

Men slept on their arms. Pickets guarded the new camp against surprise attack, but Capps made no hostile move, neither against the hill nor the old camp. Long Neck Wilson and Turkey hauled water and supplies unmolested. But still Keegan would not allow his off-duty force to return to the old camp to sleep, disturbing Capps' too easy acceptance of defeat.

The cut went rapidly. Four ribs of rock

offered the main resistance. Night and day sweating men fought rock and rattlesnakes and took lift after lift out of the cut. They lived on the ground; they fought the ground and cursed it vilely. But they moved it.

Even Derwent began to admit cautiously that there was a chance to finish the job in time to get estimates that would meet the payroll — providing, he said, the bottom of the cut didn't suddenly expand into solid rock.

By postponing payday a week Keegan knew he could beat the job even if the cut did turn to rock. McLean agreed, saying that the attitude of the men at present indicated that they might consent to a short wait for their money.

"But if they think you're trying to beat 'em out of something there'll be hell to pay," McLean said.

The long hard hours kept Keegan's men from visiting Albo's tents as much as formerly. The few who did go, oddly, had little serious trouble with Capps' men. And then late one afternoon a rumor said that Capps was planning to move in that night and retake the cut. Keegan's men were restless after dark. He himself walked about uneasily.

At ten o'clock a picket brought a message that a tall man in buckskin wanted to talk to him.

Keegan cautiously approached two dark figures beyond an outpost barricade. One was Whisper Jim and the second was Penrose Capps. Whisper laughed gently and said, "You can put the gun away, Keegan. I got Capps cooled off."

"How about yourself?" Keegan asked.

Whisper laughed again. "I knew you didn't have no money when you left Yankee Falls the other day. I told the boys so, but they didn't quite trust me."

"Suppose I *had* been carrying a payroll?" Keegan asked.

"That would have been another problem," Whisper said.

"Was that the bunch that shot my father?"

"Nope! The gang that shot up Liash was amateur toughs. One of 'em died from a wound he got that night; two of 'em have since been killed in brawls — and the others seem to have scattered or retired." He paused. "The boys we're interested in right now are the two that held up Capps. One of 'em was Boxcar Branson."

"You don't have to tell him everything," Capps growled. "That ain't why we come here."

"That's right," Whisper said. "I brought Capps over to tell you himself that he ain't going to give you trouble on your work."

"Whisper talked me out of it," Capps rumbled. "I was aiming to move you out tonight. Now he thinks he can save my hide another way."

Capps must have been taking a long chance sending part of his outfit west if he was about to go under, Keegan thought.

"Did Branson tell you something just before he died?" Keegan asked Whisper.

"He said, 'Five-four-three,' just like one word. He whispered it twice," Whisper Jim said.

"What's that mean?" Keegan asked. "Station number?"

Capps and Whisper jerked their heads toward each other.

"By God!" Capps said. "I knowed I ought to've left a few stakes on at least one job!" He went toward his horse.

"That might be a station number on the survey line," Whisper said. "Thanks, Keegan."

Keegan listened to hooves receding across the lava plain. Then he went back and told his men they could sleep in the old camp where they had tents and cots.

At dawn the next morning Stroud woke

Keegan to tell him that the four ribs in the cut had expanded into footings of solid rock. By mid-morning a rumor had taken solid root: Keegan Construction Company was flat broke and even final estimates would fall far short of meeting the payroll.

The day shift went to work after dinner in a surly mood; their efforts began to lag and Derwent raged in vain.

More rumors came to life and spread like prairie fire: Liash Keegan had died a month ago, and now his son was planning to take the final estimate check and skip the country; another said that Keegan and McLean were working together to rob the company and that Keegan was not even old Liash's son, but a crook brought in by McLean.

Nothing could stop the lies and there was no way to trace their origin.

Men began to quit. Twenty drew their money, and for once McLean paid carelessly, without argument, as if he had unlimited funds. Turkey Wilson broke the run by dragging his brother, Long Neck, out of the pay line and starting a fight with him for being a "cowardly yellow quitter!" and other things.

McLean had a hundred dollars left, but he looked as unconcerned as if he had a million.

Keegan looked at the relatively infinitesimal stretch of work where men were going through the motions only. He couldn't fire them because he couldn't pay, and if he could have paid them he knew he couldn't replace them. Track-layers were already in sight.

He went among them and explained his plight honestly. He asked them to wait an extra week for payday. Some of the old hands who had long been with Liash Keegan were willing; three fourths of the crews were not, and then Keegan knew that his request had served mainly to intensify and make more acceptable the ugly rumors.

He had almost but not quite got his miracle from the hill.

—CHAPTER TWENTY—

Derwent came to Keegan and in a voice as snarly as ever offered to forego his salary and lend three hundred dollars he had won at poker. McLean, Grieve, Stroud and a dozen more followed with similar offers.

"It's not as if you was busted," Grieve said. "We know the estimates will bring the money — but those lies that someone got started — !"

Himself cold-blooded and logical, McLean seemed to be the most enraged at the attitude of the men. "Blast their thick heads!" he said. "They ought to listen to reason!"

He proposed to show everyone the papers Liash Keegan had signed empowering his son to run the company, and that Keegan present the letter from Liash. Those two acts might quiet the rumor that Keegan was an imposter, McLean thought.

Keegan himself, more familiar than the storekeeper with the unpredictable gang spirit of men when aroused, thought the chance rather slim. But he went after the letter. It was not with the bundle of Liash's letters in the folded coat. It was not anywhere in his tent.

McLean was the only man he had even shown it to. Somehow the story leaked out and added fresh fuel to the rumor that Keegan and McLean had worked together to ruin the outfit, stealing it blind in the process.

The night shift refused to go out at six o'clock that evening. Three men had been bitten by rattlesnakes and died the night before, they said, and Keegan had had the bodies carried off and hidden. Fantastic as the story was, it took solid root and lived, even when McLean checked the timebook against men in camp, openly and loudly.

The three had been checked off as men who quit, rumor-mongers declared.

"We'll work only the day shift," Keegan said. That meant working everyone day shift, twice as many men as he could use, but he couldn't lay off anyone because he couldn't pay off.

That evening when the camp settled down to sullen muttering, with more than half the men gone to Albo's, Keegan walked down to the horse yard to think. The guard was already asleep, indicative of the spirit that had overnight replaced the cheering when Keegan had beaten Capps to the ground.

He lifted the guard bodily and set him on his feet, and when the watchman saw Keegan's eyes he stepped back in alarm. "Stay awake!" Keegan said. His voice was as low and hoarse as Whisper Jim's.

Keegan wandered out into the dusk and stood staring across the lava plain. The man who had started the rumors was the man he wanted, and he was no closer to knowing who it was than he had been the first day he rode into camp.

To deny a rumor was the surest way to introduce a rumor. Any of his men could have done that — and one had.

But right now, even if Keegan could close his fingers around the neck of the person who had directed the rumors, the act would not prevent the collapse of the company.

Only money would do that.

He stood a long time staring into the growing darkness before he could bring himself to acting on the thought that came.

Laraine came up quietly beside him.

"You haven't given up?" she asked.

In spite of the heaviness in his mind, her presence was a living, stirring pulsing in his thoughts. He smelled the fragrance of her cleanness and heard her low tones long after the words had gone into the night.

"No, I haven't quit," he said. "Suppose I pull the outfit clear and take it on west where one man with big feet is supposed to be able to kick together a mile of grade a day? Suppose I do. Then — well — you —" He couldn't fit words into thoughts.

"I know what you're trying to say. Before you came I was sure I was in love with Carson. Now I don't know. You've never said anything. That is, you've joked and tried to hide your thoughts —"

"I'll say them now!"

Keegan did, and then he said them with his arms. She pushed away gently after a moment. "I'm still not sure," she said. "I want you to know I'm not trying to play a game — I just don't know."

"Suppose I'm able to rake up the money to save the company —" Keegan said.

"I want you to win, but whether you do or not, my feelings about you wouldn't change just because you won or lost — and I'm not sure yet what my feelings are."

They stood in silence for several moments. The night guard Keegan had awakened was singing now, a song about a steamboat and a yaller gal.

"I *am* sure I want you to save the outfit,"

Laraine said. "Carson has the money to do it."

"I was thinking of him when you walked up."

"Ask him," she said.

"I have to. It's my last out."

Keegan found Carson Albo watching the wheel-of-fortune and asked the man bluntly to accompany him outside for a talk.

Albo smiled. "We may as well go to my tent and be comfortable."

They faced each other, Albo on his cot, Keegan sitting on a bale of hay. The kerosene smell of the recently lighted lantern was heavy in the tent. Albo offered Keegan a cigar and lit it for him, studying the lines of Keegan's face over the flame.

"You almost won before you got stopped at the last minute, didn't you?" Albo asked. "And now you want a loan."

"That's right. I need fifteen thousand dollars."

Albo's voice was careless. "That'll barely meet your payroll. Better make it twenty. You're going to move."

Keegan's eyes narrowed. He had detected no derision in Albo's voice, but if Albo led up to something and then tried to laugh . . .

"From what your men say in my place, I

know your work about as well as if I'd walked your job." Albo took his cigar from his mouth carefully. "I know your estimates will pay off and that only the time element has you licked at the moment." His eyes were dark and unwavering. "By the way, have you formed any ideas about who it is that's tried to ruin your outfit?"

Keegan shook his head.

Albo smiled. "You might think it's odd, but I've lain awake nights trying to work out that riddle. For a long time I was sure Capps was behind everything — and now I don't know."

"About the loan —"

"I'll give it to you," Albo said. "But first I want to tell you why, aside from the reasons that make it a sound loan." He leaned forward a little, and light gleamed on his pale forehead.

"Before you came I thought I was a cinch to marry Laraine. That doesn't mean I've given up by any means. I'm going back into contracting, Keegan — on some of that stuff out west that's supposed to be sure-fire — and then Laraine won't have any cause to look down on the business I'm in."

Albo's steady gaze was hard with challenge. "I love her, Keegan, and I intend to marry her — if and when she says she'll have me. Right now the worst thing I could do for my own case would be to refuse to help you. Some women want only winners, but Laraine isn't that kind, and if you go under you're going to have the advantage of sympathy. I can't afford to let you have any advantage, Keegan."

Their eyes held a challenge they both accepted.

Albo smiled suddenly and rose. "It's a good deal anyway."

Keegan stood up. "Have you got the money here?"

Albo shook his head. "I'll give you an order on the Yankee Falls bank and a letter to go with it."

Riding back to camp later, Keegan thought that between the check in his pocket and delivery of cash to his men lay the dangerous trip from Yankee Falls. He wondered if Albo had played deliberately upon the near-certainty that Keegan would have trouble bringing in the money. Albo must have had the cash in his camp, Keegan thought.

He went directly to McLean and told him the news. The storekeeper's face showed no expression. "I'll go with you."

"I'll go alone," Keegan said. "The way

the men are now, it'll take you and all the rest to keep the work going, and if you and I ride away together some of those dirty rumors will really look true. We can depend on somebody taking care of that little detail the minute we start."

"It's foolish to go alone," McLean said. "Not even counting the other gangs, we've got a man here that's going to try to stop you. He's got to try — or throw his hand down."

"That's what I figure," Keegan said. "He's got to come out in the open and try to stop me." His eyes were hard and speculative.

McLean held his gaze. "I can't blame you for including me in your suspicions — you have all along, I know — but I can't say that I like it either."

"Maybe we'll laugh about that later."

"Maybe," McLean said. "If you get back with the money."

Keegan assembled everyone in camp before one of the bunktents. "You'll get your money if you do the work," he told them. "I'm sending wagons to the hills for wood; I'm sending Turkey Wilson into town for two barrels of whisky and two steers to barbecue, with all the trimmings.

"We'll celebrate payday night if this job's

done!" He turned and walked away. A few men cheered. That his words would be enough to stem the ugly feeling of the men he doubted, but the message might help a little and it certainly would serve to give notice to everyone that he was riding to bring in the payroll; that he was asking to be robbed.

That was the chance he had to take, and he might as well play it to win.

He told Turkey Wilson to take one of his lighter freight wagons and set out immediately for Yankee Falls to haul the beef and whisky.

"I love a barbecue!" Turkey said. "Whisky ain't bad neither. I'll be in town when the stores open tomorrow!"

Derwent and Stroud were at Albo's, so Keegan told McLean to take charge of the camp and double the guards. He mounted Bear Trap and headed through the night for Yankee Falls.

In the first six miles he worked out the details of his plan to get the cash out of town without having to carry it himself, because he was certain that spotters would be watching the bank, men he wouldn't know if he met them face to face.

There was a grocery store next to Rowden's bank and there must be a back door to both buildings. He would arrange with the banker to have the money put in cases of canned goods, then taken into the grocery store and carried out the front door to be loaded into Turkey's wagon.

Then Keegan could come from the bank carrying nothing but his gun and himself for spotters to observe. Even Turkey wouldn't know his wagon was hauling the payroll. If the ruse was successful Keegan could pick the money up later when Turkey was out of town — or even let it ride all the way in the wagon.

That could be determined later.

Sometime during the return trip Keegan was sure he would meet the man he was after. His enemy had played the game hard and dirty right to the last; there was no reason to think he would back down now.

He would make his play and Keegan would have to call the hand.

—CHAPTER TWENTY-ONE—

In the Lava Rock Saloon across the street from the bank, Keegan dawdled with his third drink, trying not to overplay the part of a man sullen and despondent because of unsatisfactory business with a banker; trying to show no interest at all in Turkey Wilson loading stores across the street.

Turkey had his orders and one of them was not to know Keegan if he saw him. Whether or not Turkey suspected he was loading twenty thousand dollars into his wagon was something Keegan didn't know.

More than one man had watched Keegan go into the bank and come out; several of them were in the Lava Rock at the moment, still studying Keegan.

"How long does it take to get word back from Omaha?" Keegan asked the bartender, whose eyes flicked toward two idlers at the other end of the bar.

"Three, four days if they catch the train just right from here to the telegraph office," the barkeep said.

Turkey completed his work and came

across the street. The ruse might be working, Keegan thought; no one ever had heard of a teamster leaving town without having a few drinks to start him on his way. But still the sight of that unguarded wagon across the street was disturbing.

The freighter went past Keegan without a glance.

"Hauling for Capps?" someone down the bar asked Turkey. Keegan kept his eyes on the bar.

"Yep!" Turkey said.

"I heard you quit him." The voice was too casual, Keegan thought.

"I did," Turkey said. He lowered his voice so that it barely came to Keegan. "But I went back after finding out the Joe McGee outfit I'd switched to was busted."

"How come Capps is hauling clear from here?"

Keegan took a casual look at the questioner and saw a wiry, hawk-faced man with hard dark eyes.

"Special stuff for a little blowout," Turkey said. "Fill 'er up!" he told the bartender.

"You mean Capps is popping for a celebration?" The voice was cold and insistent.

Turkey laughed. "If you'd ever heard of Capps you'd know better than that. The boys are paying for this stuff!"

The teamster had done well, Keegan thought, but whether his story had stuck or not was doubtful. At any rate, the hand had to be played out.

Keegan left the bar and went to a saloon farther up the street, from which fifteen minutes later he saw Turkey swing his wagon around in the street and start out of town. Twenty thousand dollars and the Keegan Construction Company went with that wagon moving leisurely down the street.

A half-hour later, after a wait that set Keegan's nerves to jumping, he went to the red livery stable and rode slowly out of town on a rented horse.

The blue roan mare was long-limbed and moved easily, and the stable owner had assured Keegan she was a runner with plenty of endurance. Leaving Bear Trap behind might be a dead giveaway to any alert member of the payroll crowd — but there were so many "maybes" in Keegan's plan one more couldn't hurt.

He caught up with Turkey three miles out of town.

"I might have guessed it anyway," Turkey said, "but one of them fool clerks in the store poked into a case of peaches and saw a sack. I'll haul her if you say —

but you heard that sharp-eyed devil in the Lava Rock. He may get to figuring, and I don't think his friends are far away."

"I'll take it from here," Keegan said.

With the gold lashed in canvas and tied behind the saddle, be went on ahead of the freighter.

He detoured all rock formations, scanning the barren country ahead, and fighting against the relaxing heat of the noonday sun and the effects of his all-night ride.

In mid-afternoon, after topping the bulge of a small hill, he saw far out ahead of him on the plain a lone freight wagon sitting motionless. As he approached he became sure that the lean teamster on the spring seat was Long Neck Wilson.

He scowled as he considered the fact; Long Neck must have quit after all, and no telling how many more men had left the job. Lacking money to pay more than two, McLean might have had serious trouble.

The last traces of drowsiness left Keegan when he saw six riders coming toward the wagon from the west. Four were in a close group; one was a few hundred yards in the lead and one was trailing far behind.

There was no chance to go around them. He could run for Yankee Falls, but that wouldn't get the payroll into camp. He knew that Long Neck always carried a rifle under the seat. With the teamster helping and the heavy wagon as a barricade . . .

It was a chance.

He rode straight at the team. Then he saw that the wagon tongue was down and that the horses were not even hitched to the freighter.

As Keegan swung the roan mare around the leaders he could read stark, deathly terror on Long Neck's face. The teamster's adam's apple was jerking; his mouth was opening and closing without a sound. Long Neck was trying hard to convey a silent warning of some kind.

Then Keegan saw a saddled horse tied close behind the wagon, one of the black geldings Laraine generally used.

The significance of the stalled freighter came home.

He swerved the mare away so fast she stumbled. Instinctively he kicked free of the stirrups and started to unload. He heard Long Neck yell, "Look out!" and the roar of a gun from the wagon.

A split second later another shot came and a bullet grazed the long, heavy muscles in the small of Keegan's back. He heard Long Neck's horses snort in terror and plunge away.

He hit the ground and fell just as another gunshot blasted from the wagon. He heard the sodden *chunk!* of lead striking the mare, and then she was on the ground beside him. She screamed in agony. Her hindquarters were limp, her fore-feet pawing the ground as she tried to rise.

His gun free, Keegan lay close against the wounded animal. For the moment he was safe against fire from the wagon. He looked at the riders ahead. They were coming fast, but it would take them several minutes yet to reach the scene.

He twisted to look back at Long Neck. The teamster was lying low on the back of the off-wheeler and the twelve-horse team was galloping. Then Long Neck suddenly slipped off the horse and fell sprawling on the ground.

That first shot, Keegan thought, had been at Long Neck, either as a cold-blooded attempt to kill him because his usefulness as a decoy was over or in revenge for the warning yell the teamster had made as he leaped from the wagon seat.

The screams of the crippled horse grated on Keegan's nerves. But, belly down and trying to make its paralyzed hindquarters respond, the animal offered more shelter. He decided to let it live.

It might, he thought, glancing quickly toward the oncoming riders, live longer than he would.

With his gun in his left hand, he reached back and rested the weapon between the saddle and the sacks of gold. He tried a wild, blind shot at the wagon.

Quickly he shifted the gun to his right hand and strained forward to peer between the threshing legs of the horse and its weaving, snake-like neck. He saw the movement of a gun above the wagon box.

He put three quick shots below it. He saw them splinter wood and knew they had been sent almost exactly where he estimated the body of the man inside to be.

The gun above the wagon trained, spat, and lead whispered past Keegan's face. He withdrew his head. For a moment only the neck of the horse was moving and its screams were stilled.

During that uncanny interval of silence he heard a wild whoop from the nearest rider. His one chance now lay in killing the man inside the wagon and using the shelter of it for himself.

The horse began anew to paw the ground and scream. He peered under its neck once more. He saw the gun rise above the board side of the freighter. He tried to hit it with his next shot. As he pulled the trigger he knew he'd shot too high.

The quick roaring reply sent lead into the mare's weaving neck. She rolled dead on her side and pinned Keegan's left arm. He was struggling desperately to pull free when another shot ripped a furrow in the animal's hide just a few inches above his head.

Keegan's arm was coming free. He felt the scrape of flesh on rock, but he was getting loose.

The first rider was less than two hundred yards away when Keegan finally withdrew his arm. He saw that the approaching horse was nearly spent, wobbling and staggering.

Whisper Jim was on it. Five more were coming.

Flat on his stomach, Keegan raised his head and looked across the shoulder of the dead mare. The man had left the wagon and was standing at the back of it, almost completely shielded by the trembling horse he was untying.

The reins pulled free from an eyebolt and the man swung into the saddle. He was squat and burly. His mouth was twisted in a snarl. He steadied the horse and swung his gun toward Keegan.

Resting his weapon on the warm

shoulder of the dead mare, Keegan shot the man from side to side through the chest.

It was Derwent.

Even in death the superintendent's face was twisted in anger when Keegan looked down at him a few moments later, just before Whisper Jim arrived.

"I should have known all along," Keegan said.

Whisper looked at the body without expression. "So should I — after I found out him and Branson was pals from way back. They robbed Capps and hid the money right in his own grade. I found it after you gave me and Capps the tip about those figures Boxcar whispered being a station number. It took the engineers a little time to chain off the place, seeing as there wasn't a stake left."

Keegan, looked at the riders coming toward the wagon.

"Some of your folks and Capps and Albo," Whisper said. He went around the wagon. "He didn't get the skinner after all."

Long Neck was staggering toward them, holding his shoulder and cursing weakly. "Get my bottle," he said. "Under the seat."

Keegan made the teamster lie down and

started to examine his wound. Whisper called from the wagon where he was looking for Long Neck's whisky. "This thing was lined all around with hay bales. No wonder you didn't hit him."

Albo, Laraine, Stroud and McLean arrived almost at once. A few minutes later, when Laraine was putting a rough dressing on Long Neck's shoulder and trying to convince him that a pint of whisky was not a sure remedy for bullet wounds, Penrose Capps came up on his big brown saddleless workhorse.

He dismounted heavily and looked at Derwent. "I told you he was a tough nut, Keegan." He loaded his underlip with snuff. "You got him, but it's costing me five thousand I promised Whisper for getting back the money Derwent and Boxcar got off me. I told you Whisper was expensive to deal with."

McLean looked at Whisper. "How'd you know Branson was one of the pair that held Capps up?"

Whisper made his throaty, mirthless laugh and pointed to the little rolling hill from which Keegan had first seen Long Neck's wagon.

Four men had just ridden to the top of it. They were sitting their horses quietly and watching. Whisper looked at the dead mare. "You could have outrun 'em, the chances are, but if I'd known you'd gone after money —" He smiled. "Well, you made it anyway."

Whisper had played square, Keegan thought, no matter how solid he was with those outside the law. Some questions were better unanswered.

Whisper's glance said the same thing.

The men on the hill left when Stroud and McLean rode out to round up Long Neck's team. The others loaded Derwent's body into one end of the wagon and made a bed for Long Neck in the other.

They were ready to go when Turkey pulled over the low hill. He put his team into a gallop when he saw his brother's rig. He pulled alongside and climbed in to look at Long Neck when Keegan said the teamster was wounded.

"He's all right!" Turkey yelled a few minutes later. "Give him a drink!"

"He's had too much already," Laraine said.

"I'll take it then," Turkey said. He did. He wiped his mouth and looked at Keegan. "Those four gents that didn't catch you took a can of peaches apiece when they searched my wagon."

Keegan grinned. "I guess we can afford it."

Stroud exchanged his tired horse for the mount Derwent had brought along for his escape. "I'll hurry on ahead and see how Grieve is getting along running the job," he said.

With five thousand dollars in a sack tied to his saddle, Whisper Jim went east, his tired horse moving slowly. His first mission, he'd said, would be to get Bear Trap.

"And after that?" Laraine had asked.

"I may see you all farther west." He smiled and rode away.

Riding beside Laraine, with Albo on the other side, Keegan looked back and saw the tall man in buckskin go from sight beyond the little hill.

"You'll see him again," Capps said. "Whisper pops up at the most unexpected times!"

Keegan rode a while in silence. "How did it happen Derwent got so far ahead when he set the trap with the wagon?"

"I could say I suspected him, but I didn't," McLean said. "To the last minute he played smart. Early this morning he rigged up a quarrel with Stroud over the job. He pretended to get sore and said he'd take the crews to the hills to get wood for the barbecue.

"Some of us should have tumbled right then to what he was up to, but it was several hours later before Laraine got a hunch, so we all lit out and picked up a few recruits as we went."

"It's under the bridge now," Capps said. "By this time next week we'll all be headed west to make that million." He looked at Albo and Keegan riding close to Laraine and grinned at McLean.

After a while Capps said to no one in particular, "I'm sure glad I'll be one contractor with only job troubles to worry about on the next stretch."

Keegan heard him but he wasn't worried. The next job couldn't possibly be as bad as the one about finished, and work wouldn't make Albo any better-looking.

Keegan felt dusty beard stubble on his face and thought that at the moment he wasn't very good-looking himself; and then he saw Laraine watching him from the corner of her eye.

He wasn't a bit worried.

—ABOUT THE AUTHOR—

STEVE FRAZEE was born in Salida, Colorado, and for the decade 1926–1936 he worked in heavy construction and mining in his native state. He also managed to pay his way through Western State College in Gunnison, Colorado, from which in 1937 he graduated with a bachelor's degree in journalism. The same year he also married. He began making major contributions to the Western pulp magazines with stories set in the American West as well as a number of North-Western tales published in *Adventure*. Few can match his Western novels which are notable for their evocative, lyrical descriptions of the open range and the awesome power of natural forces and their effects on human efforts. *Cry Coyote* (1955) is memorable for its strong female protagonists who actually influence most of the major events and bring about the resolution of the central conflict in this story of wheat growers and expansionist cattlemen. *High Cage* (1957) concerns five miners and a woman snowbound at an isolated gold mine on top of Bulmer Peak in which the twin themes of the lust for gold and the struggle against the savagery of both the elements and human nature interplay with increasing, almost tormented intensity. *Bragg's Fancy Woman* (1966) concerns a free-spirited woman who is able to tame a family of thieves. *Rendezvous* (1958) ranks as one of the finest mountain man books and *The Way Through the Mountains* (1972) is a major historical novel. Not surprisingly, many of Frazee's novels have become major motion pictures. According to the second edition of *Twentieth Century Western Writers*, a Frazee story is possessed of 'flawless characterization, particularly when it involves the clash of human passions; believable dialogue; and the ability to create and sustain damp-palmed suspense.' His latest Western novel is *Hidden Gold* (1997).

We hope you have enjoyed this Large Print book. Other Thorndike, Wheeler or Chivers Press Large Print books are available at your library or directly from the publishers.

For more information about current and upcoming titles, please call or write, without obligation, to:

Publisher
Thorndike Press
295 Kennedy Memorial Drive
Waterville, ME   04901
Tel. (800) 223-1244

Or visit our Web site at:
www.gale.com/thorndike
www.gale.com/wheeler

OR

Chivers Large Print
published by BBC Audiobooks Ltd
St James House, The Square
Lower Bristol Road
Bath BA2 3SB
England
Tel. +44(0) 800 136919
email: bbcaudiobooks@bbc.co.uk
www.bbcaudiobooks.co.uk

All our Large Print titles are designed for easy reading, and all our books are made to last.